2/03.

1995

D0607385

Winona LaDuke

Women Changing the World

Aung San Suu Kyi
Standing Up for Democracy in Burma

Ela Bhatt
Uniting Women in India

Máiread Corrigan and Betty Williams
Making Peace in Northern Ireland

Mamphela Ramphele
Challenging Apartheid in South Africa

Marina Silva
Defending Rainforest Communities in Brazil

Rigoberta Menchú
Defending Human Rights in Guatemala

Winona LaDuke
Restoring Land and Culture in Native America

Winona LaDuke

Restoring Land and Culture in Native America

Michael Silverstone

The Feminist Press
at The City University of New York

Published by The Feminist Press at The City University of New York
The Graduate Center, 365 Fifth Avenue, New York, NY 10016
feministpress.org

First edition, 2001

Library of Congress Cataloging-in-Publication Data

Silverstone, Michael.
    Winona LaDuke : restoring land and culture in Native America / Michael Silverstone.—1st ed.
      p.   cm. — (Women changing the world)
    Includes bibliographical references and index (p.).
    ISBN 1-55861-260-2 (Hardcover : alk. paper). — ISBN 1-55861-261-0 (pbk. : alk. paper.)
    1. LaDuke, Wnona—Juvenile literature.   2. Ojibwa women—Biography—Juvenile literature.
3. Indian activists—United States—Biography—Juvenile literature.   4. Indians of North America—Government relations—Juvenile literature.   5. Environmental protection—North America—Juvenile literature.   [1. Laduke, Winona.   2. Ojibwa Indians—Biography.
3. Indians of North America—Biography.   4. Women—Biography.   5. Environmental protection.]
I. Title.   II. Series.

E99.C6 L25 2001
997'.004973'0092—dc21
[B]   2001033343

The Feminist Press is grateful to the Ford Foundation for their generous support of our work. The Feminist Press is also grateful to Mariam K. Chamberlain, Johnnetta B. Cole, Blanche Wiesen Cook, Florence Howe, Joanne Markell, and Genevieve Vaughan for their generosity in supporting this publication.

Design by Dayna Navaro
Composition by CompuDesign, Charlottesville, Virginia
Printed on acid-free paper by Transcontinental Printing
Printed in Canada

06   05   04   03   02   01   5   4   3   2   1

CONTENTS

WHAT DOES IT TAKE TO CHANGE THE WORLD?

Maybe this question sounds overwhelming. However, people who become leaders have all had to ask themselves this question at some point. They started finding answers by choosing how they would lead their lives every day and by creating their own opportunities to make a difference in the world. The anthropologist Margaret Mead said, "Never doubt that a small group of thoughtful, committed citizens can change the world; indeed it's the only thing that ever has." So let's look at some of the qualities possessed by people who are determined to change the world.

First, it takes vision. The great stateswoman and humanitarian Eleanor Roosevelt said, "You must do the thing you think you cannot do." People who change the world have the ability to see what is wrong in their society. They also have the ability to imagine something new and better. They do not accept the way things *are*—the "status quo"— as the only way things *must be* or *can be*. It is this vision of an improved world that inspires others to join leaders in their efforts to make change. Leaders are not afraid to be different, and the fear of failure does not prevent them from trying to create a better world.

Second, it takes courage. Mary Frances Berry, former head of the U.S. Commission on Civil Rights, said, "The time when you need to do something is when no one else is willing to do it, when people are saying it can't be done." People who change the world know that courage means more than just saying what needs to be changed. It means deciding to be active in the effort to bring about change—no matter what it takes. They know they face numerous challenges: they may be criticized, made fun of, ignored, alienated from their friends and family, imprisoned, or even killed. But even though they may sometimes feel scared, they continue to pursue their vision of a better world.

Third, it takes dedication and patience. The Nobel Prize–winning scientist Marie Curie said, "One never notices what has been done; one can only see what remains to be done." People who change the world understand that change does not happen overnight. Changing the world is an ongoing process. They also know that while what they do is important, change depends on what others do as well. Their original vision may transform and evolve over time as it interacts with the visions of others and as circumstances change. And they know that the job is never finished. Each success brings a new challenge, and each failure yet another obstacle to overcome.

Finally, it takes inspiration. People who change the world find strength in the experiences and accomplishments of others who came before them. Sometimes these role models are family members or personal friends. Sometimes they are great women and men who have spoken out and written about their own struggles to change the world for the better. Reading books about these people—learning about their lives and reading their own words—can be a source of inspiration for future world-changers. For example, when I was young, someone gave me a book called *Girls' Stories of Great Women,* which provided me with ideas of what women had achieved in ways I had never dreamed of and in places that were very distant from my small town. It helped me to imagine what I could do with my life and to know that I myself could begin working toward my goals.

This book is part of a series that introduces us to women who have changed the world through their vision, courage, determination, and patience. Their stories reveal their struggles as world-changers against obstacles such as poverty, discrimination, violence, and injustice. Their stories also tell of their struggles as women to overcome the belief, which still exists in most societies, that girls are less capable than boys of achieving high goals, and that women are less likely than men to become leaders. These world-changing women often needed even more vision and courage than their male counterparts, because as women they faced greater discrimination and resistance. They certainly needed more determination and patience, because no matter how much they proved themselves, there were always people who were reluctant to take their leadership and their achievements seriously, simply because they were women.

These women and many others like them did not allow these challenges to stop them. As they fought on, they found inspiration in women as well as men—their own mothers and grandmothers, and the great women who had come before them. And now they themselves stand as an inspiration to young women and men all over the world.

The women whose lives are described in this series come from different countries around the world and represent a variety of cultures. Their stories offer insights into the lives of people in varying circumstances. In some ways, their lives may seem very different from the lives of most people in the United States. We can learn from these differences as well as from the things we have in common. Women often share similar problems and concerns about issues such as violence in their lives and in the world, or the kind of environment we are creating for the future. Further, the qualities that enable women to become leaders, and to make positive changes, are often the same worldwide.

The books in this series tell the stories of women who have fought for justice and worked for positive change within their own societies. Some, like Marina Silva and Winona LaDuke, have struggled to protect the environment. In doing so, they are also struggling to protect the health and way of life of their people—the indigenous people who have lived on their land for many centuries.

One goal all these women leaders share is to promote human rights—the basic rights to which all human beings are entitled. In 1948, the United Nations adopted the Universal Declaration of Human Rights, which outlines the rights of all people to freedom from slavery and torture, and to freedom of movement, speech, religion, and assembly, as well as rights of all people to social security, work, health, housing, education, culture, and citizenship. Further, it states that all people have the equal right to all these human rights, "without distinction of any kind such as race, color, sex, language . . . or other status."

In the United States, many of these ideas are not new to us. Some of them can be found in the first ten amendments to the U.S. Constitution, known as the Bill of Rights. Yet these ideals face continual challenges, and they must be defended and expanded by every generation. They have been tested in this country, for example, by the civil rights movement to end racial discrimination and the movement to bring about equal rights for women. They continue to be tested even today by various individuals and groups who are fighting for greater equality and justice.

All over the world, women and men work for and defend the common goal of human rights for all. In some places these rights are severely violated. Tradition and prejudice as well as social, economic, and political interests often exclude women, in particular, from benefiting from these basic rights. Over the past decade, women around the world have been questioning why women's rights and women's lives have been deemed secondary to human rights and the lives of men. As a result, an international women's human rights movement has emerged, with support from organizations such as the Center for Women's Global Leadership, to challenge limited ideas about human rights and to alert all nations that "women's rights are human rights."

The following biography is the true story of a woman overcoming incredible obstacles in order to peacefully achieve greater respect for human rights in her country. I am sure that you will find her story inspiring. I hope it also encourages you to join in the struggle to demand an end to all human rights violations—regardless of sex, race, class, or culture—throughout the world. And perhaps it will motivate you to become someone who just might change the world.

Charlotte Bunch
Founder and Executive Director
Center for Women's Global Leadership
Rutgers University

You can help to change the world now by establishing goals for yourself personally and by setting an example in how you live and work within your own family and community. You can speak out against unfairness and prejudice whenever you see it or hear it expressed by those around you. You can join an organization that is fighting for something you believe in, volunteer locally, or even start your own group in your school or neighborhood so that other people who share your beliefs can join you. Don't let anything or anyone limit your vision. Make your voice heard with confidence, strength, and dedication—and start changing the world today.

The right of citizens of the United States to enjoy and use air, water, sunlight, and other renewable resources determined by the Congress to be common property shall not be impaired, nor shall such use impair their availability for use by the future generations.

—Proposed amendment to the U.S.
Constitution drafted by Walt
Bresette of the Red Cliff reservation
in northern Wisconsin

Winona LaDuke, indigenous rights activist and two-time candidate for vice president of the United States.

Chapter 1

THE VIEW FROM THE KITCHEN TABLE

What would it be like in your home if you had a new baby brother and your mother was running for vice president of the United States? Waseyabin Kapashesit knows. When she was twelve years old, she watched and helped as her mother, Winona LaDuke, spent long days in their kitchen taking care of a national campaign, a family, and a whole lot more besides.

When she wasn't traveling around the country to make speeches, Winona worked at home in the house on White Earth Indian reservation in northern Minnesota, where she and her family had lived for many years. On a typical day she would do at least four jobs at once. In her role as political candidate for election in 2000, she talked to reporters who visited or phoned. In her role as a community leader among her Native American people, the Anishinaabeg (Ojibwe), she had meetings from morning to evening with a constant stream of neighbors. She made plans and budgets with them, as she helped local farmers sell traditional Native American foods. In her role as a defender of the environment—of the earth she and her people loved—she worked to organize a national rock-and-roll tour to fund projects to preserve land and help Native American people.

Of course, throughout all this, she was also a mom. The same kitchen table that held two telephones and stacks of printed e-mails and faxes also held baby bottles and rattle rings.

Waseyabin and her younger brothers and sisters, along with Winona's partner, Kevin, helped make it possible for a family and a political campaign to thrive in the same house. When reporters called, children took messages or spoke with callers so Winona could give attention to the baby. If Winona needed to respond to a phone call herself or sit with a visitor, the family could help care for the baby, too. They would change his diapers and make sure he was comfortable. Often they pitched in to make meals for themselves and guests. As they helped each other, Winona's family also helped her accomplish important work, not only in their home, but also for their community, the nation, and even the world.

During the 2000 campaign, Winona was just forty-one years old, but she had been taking big steps to help better the world for most of her life. Through her identity as a Native American, she felt a deep connection to ancient traditions that value the bond between humans and nature. Her ability to translate such deeply held beliefs into words and projects allowed her to become an exceptional leader. When she was still a teenager, her concern about pollution and its effects on Native American people and the world led her to speak before the United Nations.

A few years later, when she graduated from college, she returned to the Indian reservation where her father was born—White Earth in Minnesota. She wanted to help the community strengthen itself and fight the effects of poverty.

Over the past twenty years, Winona's determination, intelligence, and caring have led to a steady series of remarkable accomplishments in many different roles

As an activist, she helped achieve one of the greatest victories in the history of the environmental movement—a successful fight to prevent power companies from flooding and deforesting nearly one million square kilometers in Canada.

As a writer, she published several books, including a historical novel about her Native ancestors and a study about environmental battles fought by Native people in the United States and Canada.

As a public speaker and fund-raiser, she organized and headlined four tours with musicians such as the Indigo Girls and Bonnie Raitt to raise more than $600,000 for projects to help Native American communities.

As a founder and director of the White Earth Land Recovery Project, she helped the people of her tribe begin to recover lost land and restore their traditional harvesting, crafts, and culture.

As an environmental activist, she served as one of the directors of Greenpeace, one of the biggest organizations fighting to protect the environment from pollution.

As an advocate for women, she helped found an international organization of women from indigenous cultures and spoke before the United Nations World Conference on Women in Beijing, China.

And as a national political leader, she was nominated twice by the Green Party to run for vice president of the United States.

Growing up as a shy and self-conscious girl, who often faced prejudice in her small hometown in Oregon, Winona had no idea that she was destined to do any of these things. All those big accomplishments would have seemed unimaginable to her as she went about her daily life at school and at home.

How did this quiet but serious young person make the journey to become a dynamic and self-assured leader? How did she develop the powerful tools of modern leadership while maintaining an unbroken connection to the spirit of Native American traditions?

Some of the answers can be discovered in Winona's early years of learning and activism in high school and college. Looking back even further, though, we can see the roots of her unique life in the contrasting worlds of her two very different parents.

Chapter 2
TWO CULTURES

Winona LaDuke is the daughter of two dynamic people from backgrounds that could hardly be more different. Her father was raised on an Indian reservation in northern Minnesota; her mother grew up in New York City. In spite of their differences, they shared a common willingness to travel across borders in order to learn about the world.

Betty Bernstein, Winona's mother, came from a Jewish neighborhood in the South Bronx. As a young girl, she developed an interest in art. From the start, Betty wanted to document the lives of working people. She used her talent as an artist to draw and paint scenes of the everyday life around her: sidewalk vendors, the elderly, children, and poor people. Her artwork led to scholarships, and her boldness and curiosity about the world led her to explore places that people in her family could scarcely imagine.

In the summer of 1950, when she was a teenager about to enter college, Betty wanted to go out and see what the world was really like. She traveled across the country, visiting the Midwest and the South, including the cities of St. Louis, Memphis, and New Orleans. She had saved some money, and she made it last by staying in dormitories and doing farm labor along the way as a harvester.

On her travels, Betty learned a lot about the lives of poor people and people of other races. In the South at that time, African Americans were legally barred from sharing the same parks, restaurants, hotels, and bathrooms as whites. With her dark complexion, darkened further by the sun, Betty was often mistaken for an African American. She accepted this identity because she wanted to experience for herself the difficulties that African Americans faced.

Several years later, in 1953, she decided to study art at the Instituto de Allende in San Miguel de Allende, Mexico. She was especially interested in the lives of the poor farmers of that country, many of whom were Indians. Even after she was no longer a student, she continued to live in Mexico, staying with an Otomie Indian family. She worked there for a year painting murals in the one-room schoolhouses of indigenous, or

Winona's parents, Betty Bernstein of New York City and Vincent LaDuke from White Earth Indian reservation in Minnesota, met and married in the late 1950s. Here they are pictured with Winona, born in 1959.

Indian, people. When Betty returned to the United States, she had a greater understanding of other ways of life and other cultures. She had seen the world in a bigger way, and it had changed her.

Betty met Vincent LaDuke in New York City in 1958. In him, she found someone who shared her own interest in making society fairer for African Americans, Native Americans, and others. Both Betty and Vincent were willing to do the hard work of taking unpopular stands and trying to convince

Who are American Indians?

The term "American Indian" has its origins in the misunderstandings of the first Europeans to travel to the New World. Because they were unaware of the existence of the Americas, they believed that their travels across the Atlantic Ocean had brought them to India. Christopher Columbus and others assumed that the people he encountered were therefore "Indians." Due to his error, all non-Europeans from the ancient civilizations of the Americas fell under this single inaccurate term.

Of course, the truth is much different and more complicated. In different regions of the Americas, civilizations and tribal groups had formed over thousands of years, all with different cultures and ways of life. In North America, for instance, the differing environments of the Arctic, the Great Plains, and the deserts of the Southwest led to several hundred distinct tribes and nations. They include the Inuit of the Arctic, the Ojibwe of the Subarctic, the Kwakiutl of the Northwest, the Pomo of California, the Klamath of the Rockies, the Pawnee of the Plains, the Seminole of the Southeast, the Iroquois of the Northeast, and the Hopi of the Southwest, to name only a few.

Though the all-encompassing term "American Indian" originated in a misunderstanding, many of the people it refers to currently accept and use it. Others prefer more technically accurate terms such as "Native American" or "indigenous." Still others prefer to identify individuals by the names of their particular tribes.

The use of a certain name or term has an important impact on how people are viewed by others outside their group. It also affects the way members of a group see themselves. This is why it is important to be conscious of the terms used and make sure they meet with the approval of the people spoken about, or spoken with.

others to join the struggle for fairness. Their political ideas drew them together, but Winona also notes that when they met, her parents were two confident and attractive young people. Her mother had an independence that was unusual in women in the 1950s. Winona's handsome father likewise carried himself with a sense of ambition and purpose. Winona says she is not surprised that two such distinctive people would find each other.

Winona's father, Vincent "Sun Bear" LaDuke (who died in 1992), was a member of the Mississippi Band of the Anishinaabeg, a Native American tribe also known as the Ojibwe or Chippewa Indians. The Anishinaabeg are inhabitants of the White Earth reservation in northern Minnesota, where Vincent grew up in the traditions and culture of his tribe. Still, like many, he had dreams and goals that took him beyond the reservation.

He made his living primarily as an actor, playing small supporting roles as an Indian in movies known as Westerns. These films depicted the settlement of the American West by white people, and often showed battles between them and Native Americans. When Vincent wasn't working as an actor, he worked to get attention and support to improve conditions for Native peoples.

When he met Winona's mother, Vincent was in New York selling wild rice grown at White Earth. Before that he had been in Washington, D.C., where his goal was to influence representatives in Congress to fund improved housing for Native Americans. On his journey to Washington, Vincent had tried to raise public awareness about the poverty and lack of educational opportunities on reservations. In a success-

What is a reservation?

When Europeans arrived in North America two hundred years ago, tribes and nations thousands of years old inhabited most of the continent. In the years that followed, the Native population was largely displaced. Many were forced to leave their traditional lands and many others were killed by direct attack, epidemics, or starvation.

It is difficult to imagine the scale of catastrophe that this displacement represented for Native peoples. Gradually, as the U.S. population grew, farmers, homesteaders, and the government itself took possession of what had been tribal land. Native peoples who survived often made written agreements with the U.S. government called treaties, which were meant to resolve conflicting claims over the use and ownership of tribal land taken by non-Indians. These agreements gave tribes hunting or fishing rights to some areas and possession of more limited parcels of land called reservations.

These tracts of land remain today. Native Americans continue to live there, but conditions are very difficult. Because reservations are separated from towns and cities where schools and jobs are found, they are among the poorest areas in the United States. Rates of alcoholism, untreated mental illness, crime, and domestic violence there are high.

Reservations are run by Tribal Councils, composed of Native Americans, and by the Bureau of Indian Affairs (BIA), which is part of the U.S. government. In the 1800s the BIA made many decisions without consulting the tribes, and Native people lost the right to determine their own way of life. In recent years, reservations and tribes have fought for political rights to self-governance.

Because reservations can make laws that in some cases differ from those of surrounding states or counties, some tribes have been able to operate gambling casinos and sell cigarettes without taxes. This has meant more money for tribes, but has brought other problems as well.

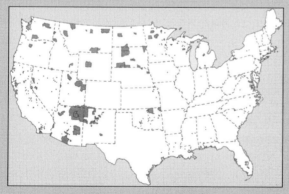

This map shows the locations of Native American reservations in the United States today. Because Native tribes were driven west by European settlers, most reservations are in the western states.

ful bid to make everyone aware of the problems, he had hitchhiked cross-country from Nevada in traditional Native clothing, including a feathered headdress. He talked to people about the difficult conditions on reservations and was interviewed and photographed throughout the journey.

Betty and Vincent's life together began in one leap. Having met and recognized in each other a similar spirit of adventure, they left New York together in a van. From the city, they drove to the White Earth reservation in Minnesota and stayed with Vincent's mother, Judith LaDuke, in the two-room cabin where she had raised six children.

For six weeks, Betty followed Vincent as he hunted, trapped, skinned, and cleaned deer, beaver, rabbit, and raccoon. She got to know members of his family and began to learn about the Anishinaabeg way of life. She learned what it was like to harvest wild rice from a canoe and what it was like to survive by hunting animals. However, once the snow began to fall, Betty and Vincent had difficult decisions to make.

Betty's family did not accept or even understand her desire to marry Vincent LaDuke. Betty's parents had immigrated to the United States in the 1920s, seeking a better way of life. Her mother's family came from Poland, and her father's from the Ukraine. Like many Jews of their era, they fled the violence and harsh economic conditions in Eastern Europe that arose from anti-Jewish prejudice.

As immigrants in a new country, Sam, Betty's father, worked as a housepainter, and Helen, her mother, worked in a factory. They struggled to put down roots, and like many newcomers from Europe, they had little knowledge or understanding of indigenous people in the United States. Betty explained, "For them, the world was either Jewish or Christian, and they had no concept of what is an Indian." They worried about their daughter marrying into a completely unfamiliar culture, and one that faced strong prejudice from many European Americans.

But Betty and Vincent knew they wanted to start a life together. Still, Betty was sure that she did not want to live at White Earth year round. "Living off the land was a full-time, tough existence, and I could not see devoting myself to this reality," she wrote recently. So the couple decided to begin their new life in a new place.

Helen Bernstein was a loving grandmother to Winona and offered an inspring example of someone who spoke out against unfairness. In this picture, taken in Los Angeles, Winona is three years old.

They moved to California, to a Native American neighborhood in East Los Angeles. Vincent continued to work in movies, and Betty went to college to become an art teacher. In a very short time, she learned that she was expecting a baby. This made her even more determined to become a teacher. Vincent's income from acting was not something a family could count on as their only source of money.

Winona was born on August 18, 1959, at Los Angeles Community Hospital. After Winona's birth, the LaDuke and Bernstein families each lent their support. Soon Judith LaDuke came from Minnesota to live for six months with Winona and her parents. After that, Helen Bernstein stayed with the young family. Helen's example would come to be an important influence on Winona. As a young woman, Helen had been involved in the pocketbook workers' union. This group fought for the fair treatment of workers at the factory where she was employed making purses. In the 1930s and 1940s, she went out to raise money and support for organizations that opposed the dictators then ruling Europe and tried to help victims of war. Helen's courage, intelligence, and caring were eventually passed on to her daughter and granddaughter.

Another important influence on Winona was her father, who continued to be involved in Native American life. When Winona was still a toddler, Vincent started a magazine called *Many Smokes*, which reported the news of different tribes around the country. The Los Angeles area was a good place to gather information. Many Native Americans came to live there from surrounding states such as Washington, Oregon, Arizona, New Mexico, and Nevada. To promote his magazine, Vincent traveled with Winona and Betty to powwows, sweat lodges, and tribal events at various reservations.

Winona's mother encouraged and supported opportunities for her daughter to experience tribal

Winona learned about Native American culture and traditions through her father, Vincent. An activist and organizer on behalf of Native Americans, he also taught his daughter about the many problems facing indigenous people.

What is a powwow?

A powwow is a festival-like gathering held to strengthen and celebrate community among Native American people. The word "powwow" comes from the Narraganset term *Powwaw*, referring to a person who conducted or led rituals and ceremonies. Over the past two hundred years, the word entered the English language and came to refer to any social gathering where rituals or decision making takes place.

Contemporary Native American powwows feature traditional dance and ceremonies. Though some are strictly for members of particular tribes, others may be open to outsiders, including non-Native participants. Most powwows share common features, including an opening parade (called the Grand Entry), honor songs, and invocations. Often a powwow will involve dance competitions in different styles, such as Traditional Dance, Grass Dance, Straight Dance, and Fancy Dance. The purposes of the dances vary. Some are to tell stories, others are to display elaborate costumes and skills.

Dancers and spectators participate in a 1962 powwow in Ottawa, Illinois, conducted by Chief White Eagle, religious leader of the Winnebago tribe.

In recent years, powwows have served an important role in helping Native Americans preserve heritage and culture. Increasingly, Native Americans who live and work in urban communities have found ways to commute on weekends and holidays to reservations to take part in traditional life. Beginning in the 1950s, intertribal powwows in various regions of the United States also served an important role in building the American Indian rights movement.

ceremonies and culture. It was important to both her parents that Winona have this connection. She began early with visits to White Earth and other Native American communities. Before she could walk, her father took her horseback riding. She celebrated her third birthday on a Navajo reservation in Arizona. These early experiences would leave a powerful impression on Winona that would last all her life.

Her memories of this time are especially important to her, because soon everything Winona was used to would change. Though they shared many common interests, Betty and Vincent LaDuke began to grow apart. They separated and divorced when Winona was five years old. Vincent would continue his political work and would also become a popular author and founder of the Bear Tribe, a community for Indians and non-Indians. Betty had become an art instructor and continued to paint and draw. In 1964 she left East L.A. with Winona to begin a life in a very different kind of place—Ashland, Oregon.

Chapter 3
EARLY YEARS

Most of the families living in Ashland, Oregon, in 1964 were white. Mexican Americans, Asian Americans, and other people of color lived over the mountain from the town. That's where the Klamath Indian reservation was and the neighborhoods of poor, working families. This division of people by race affected how Winona felt about herself as a child.

"When I was little, I used to be made fun of a lot," Winona recalls. From first grade on, she came to think of herself as an outsider—someone who couldn't be fully accepted. She guessed that people didn't like her because of something she was doing wrong—or something wrong with her.

But there was nothing wrong with Winona, though there was something different about her. Her skin and hair were darker than most of her classmates'. "I grew up knowing I was dark because I was an Indian," Winona remembers. "I was the darkest person in my school. You just know that you don't fit in," she explains. Still, as a child, she couldn't understand why it had to be that way. Winona didn't have a word for it at the time, but she was experiencing racism.

Despite feeling separate from many of her classmates, Winona made a number of close friends in Ashland with whom she shared her sense of humor

What is racism?

Racism is a way of thinking that places higher or lower values on people according to their racial characteristics.

At best, racism is mistaken and foolish. Generalizations based on race are almost always inaccurate or untrue. Even the idea of racial categories suggests something more exact than can be found in the real world. In the early twentieth century, those attempting to make a science of racial identification measured facial features and the shape of ear lobes and cataloged hundreds of thousands of people, but in fact could come up with no classification rules that precisely defined a racial group.

At worst, racism encourages the grouping of people based on "desirable" and "undesirable" characteristics, and the denial of equal rights or opportunities based on these groupings. It can also lead some groups to view other groups as undeserving of basic rights. Members of oppressed groups can mistakenly apply this kind of harmful thinking to themselves and each other.

In Germany, under Hitler, racist ideas led to hatred and mass executions of people for being members of particular ethnic or racial groups. One such group was the Jews.

Throughout the history of the United States, race has determined political rights. African Americans could legally be bought and sold as slaves until the 1860s. As late as 1950, laws in thirty states forbade marriage between two people of different races.

The taking of traditional lands belonging to Native Americans was also the result of racism. Their right to their land and property was not respected because of the attitude of superiority that European Americans had towards indigenous peoples.

Though many of the most obviously racist laws have been struck down or changed in the United States, some of the most harmful effects of racism continue. Racial discrimination in education, housing, and employment still exists and leads to lack of opportunity. Because opportunities are scarce, long-term poverty tends to be a fact of life for members of particular racial or ethnic groups.

and her appreciation of fun. What's more, she liked to read and learn. This allowed her to be happy even when some students and teachers acted in ways that made her feel left out.

Another important source of support for Winona was her family. Shortly after moving to Ashland, her mother married Peter Westigard, an entomologist (a scientist who studies insects). Soon afterward, Winona's half brother, Jason Westigard, was born, and she became a devoted and caring big sister.

Winona credits her stepfather as well as her parents Betty and Vincent for both teaching her to believe in herself and being good examples. Peter Westigard worked hard, and he believed work was something done to serve others. For instance, he applied his skills as an entomologist to finding natural ways to stop the insects that attack pear trees. The research took years, and he did it to save the pears, Winona observes, not to advance his career.

Winona was also aware of her parents' involvement in political movements for civil rights and social justice and against war. Both Betty and Vincent had worked to help American Indians recover their land and get support from the U.S. government. Betty had also gone to the Poor People's March on Washington and worked to support farmworkers in the 1960s. Her parents' political beliefs influenced Winona. Even as a child, she cared about working for fairness in the world.

"My parents never said, 'Go out and look out for number one,'" Winona recalls. "I never heard that one from my house. I always heard, 'Go out and do the right thing.' That's all I ever heard. And it wasn't preached to me. It was done by example, because my parents were like that."

Sometimes doing the right thing led her into conflict with people in authority. Once a teacher who had served in the military was telling Winona's class about why it was good that the United States was fighting a war in Vietnam. Winona felt the war was wrong and needed to say so.

Winona, age thirteen, shares a happy moment at the Oregon coast with her half brother, Jason Westigard, age two.

What was the civil rights movement?

The freeing of slaves after the Civil War did not end the injustices that have affected African Americans in the United States. Instead, it marked the beginning of a legal system of segregation (keeping people separated by race), which kept the former slaves from benefiting from full participation in society.

Separate schools, restaurants, drinking fountains, and even sections of trains and buses kept African Americans and whites apart in many parts of the nation.

The unfairness of this led to questions and protests. In 1954 the United States Supreme Court ruled that it was not fair for a town to maintain separate schools for people of different races. This legal victory helped inspire the civil rights movement. African Americans and others who agreed with their cause used boycotts, petitions, and other means so that all people, regardless of race, could enjoy the same rights and opportunities.

Some of the leaders of this movement were ordinary people such as Rosa Parks, a woman from Montgomery, Alabama. She showed her courage by refusing to obey the law that required African Americans to give up their seats to white bus passengers. Later in the 1960s, the civil rights movement achieved such visible highlights as the March on Washington led by Dr. Martin Luther King, Jr., and changes in the law such as the new Voting Rights Act.

The civil rights movement may have begun as a struggle for equality by African Americans, but its successes opened the door for other groups to seek solutions to the problems affecting them. Mexican Americans, American Indians, gay rights activists, feminists, and others can be said to have built on a tradition established by the civil rights movement.

It was not easy for her to disagree with a teacher. Her experiences in school had taught her not to draw attention to herself. Even so, she said what she thought, although it meant contradicting the teacher.

Winona's mother came to school the next day to make sure Winona and her ideas were treated fairly. Winona said this experience left a big impression on her. "It's really powerful for a kid when you get the big guns—like Mom—to back you up," she observed. Getting that support helped her know she was a

In June 1968 close to 60,000 Americans gathered in Washington, D.C., to demand an end to poverty and economic injustice. The Poor People's March was the idea of Dr. Martin Luther King, Jr., the civil rights leader, who wanted to unite people of all races in the fight against poverty. His assassination in April 1968 caused many to join the march in a show of support for his ideals..

person whose ideas mattered. It also helped her feel how the support of others could give her confidence even if she was taking an unpopular stand. And there were other times when Winona had to stand up for what she thought was right on issues in the classroom.

In eighth grade, one of Winona's teachers used to award students either "points" or "bad potatoes." As Winona remembers it, "Boys always got points and we never got points. The girls got bad potatoes."

One day, when the teacher was out of the room, Winona went to the podium where the teacher's grade book was and erased all the bad potatoes. She didn't just erase her own, she erased all of them in the book. That way she thought it was fair to everyone.

And that's where the story ends. The teacher never confronted or accused her. What's more, no one told the teacher that she had erased the potatoes, though everyone had seen her do it. Maybe her classmates

What is the American Indian rights movement?

Though the U.S. government has made hundreds of treaties with Native American peoples granting them lands and protections, it has not always honored these agreements. Native American rights to live, hunt, and fish in particular areas have often been ignored when business or government has wanted to use the land for other purposes. By the 1960s, many Native Americans felt that the time had come to protest and to try to reverse the centuries of unfair treatment.

Indian leaders from many tribes met in Chicago in 1961. Soon after, the National Indian Youth Council was formed. With the help of this organization, Native Americans moved to assert their rights to traditional lands and waters and to stop the pollution that threatened their people.

One public protest got worldwide attention. In 1969 more than five hundred Native Americans occupied Alcatraz Island in San Francisco Bay, famous as the site of an abandoned federal prison. By taking over the island, they reminded people that the land originally belonged to them.

By 1973 many Native Americans were ready to express a new independence. That year nearly three hundred Oglala Sioux gathered at the Pine Ridge reservation in South Dakota at the village of Wounded Knee—site of a dreadful massacre of Sioux by U.S. troops in 1890. The Sioux declared that Wounded Knee was part of a separate nation.

Government agents immediately surrounded the area. After a seventy-one-day standoff, a truce was negotiated. Though two protesters were killed and 120 were arrested, the action succeeded in focusing new attention on the struggles of Native Americans to reclaim land and rights.

Native American protesters give the Red Power salute moments after being removed from Alcatraz Island in June 1971. The salute was a symbol of unity among people of different tribes all fighting to restore land and rights to Native Americans.

were just relieved that the bad potatoes were gone, Winona suggests. Maybe they were also surprised that a girl in the class had the courage to stick up for what was fair.

In telling this story, Winona wants to be clear that she wasn't very outspoken as a student in Ashland. She could state her mind on occasion, but didn't have the social confidence to show off or be brash. Still, she says, "I must have been quite gutsy to do that."

In high school Winona discovered new sources of strength and began to come into her own. In addition to enjoying accomplishments as a student, she found success as a member of her school's debating team. Through debate, she also found new friends.

Debate is a kind of game or sport played with words. Like other sports, it involves two teams trying to win a contest by scoring points, while trying to keep the other team from doing the same thing. Instead of using a ball, debaters use arguments. In a debate, the teams take opposing positions on a particular topic. High school debate teams argue about a single topic all year. In some matches they are asked to agree with a statement, in others they have to disagree. One of the years Winona was on the team, the statement was "Resolved: The United States should have a national energy policy."

To succeed, a debater must build a convincing argument, based on accurate information. Winona and her debate partner, Lynne Abernathy, did a lot of research on energy at the library. They learned technical and scientific facts and gathered statistics and opinions from many sources. Winona's school had a

Visiting the Southwest on a high school internship, Winona prepares to order a meal at the Uranium Café in Grants, New Mexico. The café takes its name from the uranium mining in the area.

tradition of excellence in debate contests. Winona, Lynne, and their teammates helped the school win more trophies to add to its large collection.

Winona's success was due to both talent and hard work. She spent long hours developing her speaking skills. She learned ways to find information in a library to support her arguments. She also practiced listening for details and responding thoughtfully and quickly to an opponent. One thing that helped her was her talent for remembering specific quotes, numbers, and facts. Later in life, an admiring observer would describe her as an "animated encyclopedia."

Winona's overall comfort with debate can be traced back to early experiences. She had grown up in a family that was passionate about ideas and politics. She remembers many heated discussions at the dinner table about current events, such as the Watergate hearings and the war in Vietnam, when she was a child. Her mother recalls that the participants in these family discussions "didn't always agree, and it was very good to just battle with ideas." Betty adds that Winona "was never one to shy away from that."

While high school debate was fun, it also provided valuable preparation for the work that Winona would do as an adult. In years to come she would have special opportunities because of her skills with research, presenting information, and making strong arguments. "I can trace my skills with these things directly back to debate," Winona states. She advises young people that one of the most valuable skills they can develop is the ability to do research and present information in a convincing way.

Although Winona met many people through debate, when she looks back on high school now, she concludes that she was not one of the popular kids. It was not that she was disliked, it was that she was ignored. As evidence, she points to the fact that she didn't have a date for the junior or senior prom, which, she says, is "a pretty good indicator."

However, sometimes what seems hurtful at the time can turn out to have been helpful in the long run. Being left out meant she didn't have to change herself constantly to keep up with the popular kids. She was free to be herself and she was comfortable with who she was.

Now that she is a grown-up woman with a husband and children and many lifelong friends, Winona sees the difficulties of her teenage years as having had a positive outcome: "I think around the eighth grade I actually figured out that I did not want approval from some imaginary clique of girls. And so I had this group of friends who enjoyed ourselves in whatever we did."

Winona's best friends, including her debate partner, Lynne, and her friend Liz Cecil, who had come to Oregon from New York, encouraged each other in their development from girls into young women. They spent a lot of time doing things like being in the woods, hiking, camping, and simply hanging out together, enjoying each other's company.

"I think that was a healthy thing in the end," Winona says now, "because over time I still have great friendships with a number of women from that time. And to this day I count as blessings that I have some of these really remarkable women as my

As the time approached for Winona to leave for college, her mother, Betty, created this painting, called Winona, the Parting. Guided by an inner spirit, which Betty depicts as a bird, Winona (at right) moves into adulthood and independence.

Why and how are girls often shortchanged in school?

According to a 1992 study by the American Association of University Women called *How Schools Shortchange Girls*, males and females are often treated differently in today's schools and universities. Though most teachers do not intend it, their behavior in the classroom often discourages girls and young women from participating equally with their male counterparts.

There are a number of ways that teacher behavior can discourage girls from developing confidence. For example, teachers have been found to ask questions and then look only at male students for a response. Often teachers praise female students for waiting patiently. Boys, however, receive positive teacher attention when they call out answers. According to researchers, teachers listen to boys when they call out comments, but usually ask girls to wait their turn.

The effects of gender discrimination can be harmful. Compared with men, women are much less likely to go into science, mathematics, and technology careers. They are, however, more likely than men to hold low-paying jobs in fields such as clerical work and retail sales.

In order for classroom conditions to improve for girls, a number of things need to happen. Teachers need to become more aware of behaviors that lower girls' confidence and that signal that girls are not expected to succeed. They also need to notice ways they may be favoring males at the expense of their female students.

friends—like twenty different friends around the country—who are all really independent, really dynamic women in their own communities."

As the end of high school approached, Winona began to make plans for her future. In spite of her high test scores and excellent grades, her guidance counselor advised her to apply to a vocational or technical school. Winona wasn't sure why she had been given this advice—but at that time, school officials commonly believed that girls and Native Americans were less likely to succeed in college. Winona disregarded the counselor's advice. In fact, she was determined to prove it wrong.

She applied to the three universities she felt had the most difficult entrance requirements: Harvard, Yale, and Dartmouth. Each one accepted her. In the end, she chose to go to Harvard because it was the school nearest to a big city. "I also think I went to Harvard because they told me I couldn't," Winona once told a reporter. At the age of seventeen, she was ready to leave her hometown behind and become part of a bigger world.

Chapter 4

DISCOVERING IDENTITY AND STRENGTH

Lowell House, built in 1930, is a typical student dormitory at Harvard. The university was founded in 1636 and is one of the oldest and wealthiest institutions of higher education in the United States.

For Winona to go from her small-town Oregon high school to Harvard University involved a big adjustment. Harvard is a wealthy school known for its famous graduates. Many of its students have gone on to hold high positions in business and government. Among them are U.S. Presidents John F. Kennedy and Franklin D. Roosevelt.

Because of this history some students at Harvard expect their school to focus on training them to go out and run the world. But not everyone there has always felt comfortable with that goal. One group that saw things differently in Winona's day was a campus American Indian organization. Winona remembers that shortly after her arrival at school, members of this group came knocking on her door to invite her to join them. She did and her life took a new path.

It was a powerful experience for Winona to join together with others and not have to be alone in her identity as a person with a tribal heritage. It made her feel supported in a sense of belonging.

Before the 1960s it was difficult for nonwhite students and immigrants to gain entrance to colleges and universities such as Harvard. Many top schools had policies that favored white students from well-established families. In the 1970s, however, the pres-

The American Indian student organization at Harvard met frequently so that members could get to know each other, offer each other support, and discuss issues facing Native Americans inside and outside the university. Winona stands second from the left, in the front row.

sure of public opinion—and new laws—made these schools work harder to attract students from different ethnic and racial backgrounds. African American students, Native American students, Latino students, and others entered Harvard and other elite schools in small, but increasing, numbers.

This opening of opportunity brought new problems with it. In the 1970s, it could feel difficult and even lonely to be a "minority student"—someone of nonwhite, non-Christian, or non-European background—on a mostly white campus. Being different both from other students and also from family and friends back home made attending a university such as Harvard a lot like being a foreigner in an unfamiliar country.

For this reason, minority students came together to form organizations like the one Winona joined, to help each other succeed and to face common issues as a group.

Winona explains that her organization had three main goals: The first goal was helping Native American students stay in school. This was important, she says, "because there's such a high drop-out rate." Adjusting to college life is difficult, and it can be especially hard to handle all the challenges if a student feels different and alone. Belonging gave Winona and other students support and fellowship that raised their spirits.

The second goal of this organization was to respond to things that were happening on campus. Because many people at Harvard, like people in her hometown of Ashland, were unfamiliar with Native Americans, they sometimes said or did things—knowingly or unknowingly—that Native Americans felt were disrespectful. "It might be the case of a campus museum having sacred objects that it shouldn't have—such as bones taken from burial grounds, or professors who are making racist remarks," Winona recalls. Responding to these kinds of offenses as a group helped Native American students find a voice to answer injustices in their daily life.

As its third goal, the group looked at the problems of the Native American community in the world beyond the gates of Harvard. When Winona began to do this as well, she discovered what would grow to become her life's work.

Some students who were not Native Americans were also concerned with these problems. They formed the Native American Solidarity Committee, which included all kinds of people interested in supporting the rights of American Indians. In Winona's first semester, the committee brought a speaker named Jimmie Durham to campus. Jimmie Durham was a well-known Cherokee artist, activist, and member of the International Treaty Council, a group that kept track of agreements and promises made between governments and indigenous peoples. His talk would have an enormous impact on Winona's thinking.

"Basically, he said, 'There's no such thing as an Indian problem—it's a government problem,'" Winona remembers. This simple statement caused things to fall suddenly into place in her mind. Native peoples had thrived in North America for 30,000 years before the arrival of Europeans. They had never asked to be part of the United States or Canada. The problems had come in the past few hundred years, when the U.S. and Canadian governments put themselves on top of tribal nations.

Because the source of the problems was outside the Native American community, Native Americans alone could not solve them. Government had to act differently. It would have to understand the importance of protecting the earth, which is the belief most important to tribal peoples. Similarly, the problem of racism, which Winona experienced with her classmates in Ashland, had only one solution. It would not be solved by Winona trying to act differently or be someone else. The people with racist attitudes and practices would have to be the ones to change.

Jimmie Durham's words gave Winona tools to understand what was really happening in the world, why, and what needed to be done. She was inspired both by his words and by the work of organizations like the International Treaty Council. She asked Jimmie if she could go to work for him as a research assistant, and he agreed. Part of her job was to look through old treaties and find out exactly what promises the United States had made to tribal peoples. Jimmie recognized Winona's commitment and skill, and he helped connect her with other groups doing work to protect the rights of Native Americans.

As it turned out, Winona was in a good place to find information. Like many college students, she had a job on campus. Hers was at the library at the School of Government. In addition to doing research there, she helped set up visits by different speakers. One day, government scientists gave a presentation she never forgot.

These scientists helped make nuclear weapons for the military. One of the things they did was think about how much wars cost the government in money. "I was totally astonished and flabbergasted that people actually considered cost in their analysis and they had an evaluation of a human life. I remember it was $237,000. How could they figure that?" Winona recalls. To her, human life was much more valuable than any amount of money.

As Winona uncovered more information about the government's nuclear weapons program, she ran across something that particularly disturbed her. It had to do with uranium, which is used in making bombs.

A government scientific journal was describing the problem of radioactive pollution caused by mining uranium. It said that human beings should not live in areas with uranium mines.

What is uranium and how is it dangerous?

Uranium is a very heavy, radioactive metal found in certain minerals, or rocks, that can be mined from the earth. A radioactive material is one that continually breaks down, giving off atomic particles and radiation that can damage the cells of living things.

For this reason, exposure to radioactive materials such as uranium is very dangerous. Over time it can cause radiation poisoning, which has symptoms that include fever, rash, bleeding gums, and hair loss, and which can result in death. Exposure to radiation has also been known to cause various forms of cancer.

In 1945 scientists discovered how to use uranium to make a bomb so powerful that it could destroy an entire city. The bomb employs a process called atomic fission. Its tremendous power can create an instant fireball many thousands of degrees hot, which can vaporize or melt everything for miles around. It also produces huge clouds of radioactive dust and debris, which can rain down and settle over a vast area. This is what caused the destruction and suffering in the Japanese cities of Hiroshima and Nagasaki when the United States bombed them in August 1945.

After World War II, scientists found other uses for the power of uranium. They designed engines that ran on the heat made from a controlled fission reaction. These engines could run power plants and provide power to ships and submarines.

One problem with radioactive materials is that their use always creates poisonous by-products. For example, when uranium is mined, the rock taken from the ground to the surface is radioactive. The mining area becomes contaminated, and the miners are exposed to radioactive gas and dust.

As radioactive materials in a power plant age, they eventually lose some of their radioactivity and have to be replaced. There is no safe way to dispose of radioactive material. Even when radioactive waste is buried underground, it can contaminate water and soil and make areas uninhabitable for thousands of years.

The cooling towers at Three Mile Island nuclear power plant are a reminder of the dangers involved in harnessing nuclear fission to produce energy. When a leak developed in the plant's cooling system in 1979, its core overheated, and radioactive gases escaped into the environment. An even larger disaster was narrowly avoided.

What upset Winona was that most of the world's uranium comes from Native communities. "So what's that mean?" she asks. "It means probably they shouldn't be living there." But the U.S. government continued to promote uranium mining, and most people who lived nearby didn't realize how dangerous it was. This information was all in government documents, but it was hard to find and was written in language that most people couldn't understand.

Winona knew she could help, and that her help would be especially valuable to Native American groups such as Jimmie Durham's. She explains that what she did involved "taking the documents that were written in 'government-ese,' as I called it, and translating it to common English or making it accessible, and then people would translate it into Navajo."

In high school Winona had shown certain talents for understanding science, for debate, and for writing. Working on government documents gave her a way to use these skills to contribute to causes she cared about. Winona had found a way to make a difference in the world. Making important information plainly available in an accurate and usable form can be a very powerful action. In Winona's case it was an action that led to her speaking before the United Nations (UN) when she was eighteen years old.

In 1977, in Geneva, Switzerland, the UN held a conference to look at how the rights of indigenous peoples could be better respected. The UN is an organization that nations use to make decisions and solve problems that go beyond any single country's borders. This was the first time that indigenous peoples

What was the Iroquois Confederacy?

It is widely stated that the founding of the United States of America brought a new kind of government into being—a representative democracy, which united the thirteen original colonies.

In fact, some of the forms and ideas that went into the new U.S. government came from a Native American system of government called the "Six Nations" or "Iroquois Confederacy." The six nations were a group of northeastern tribes: the Mohawk, Oneida, Onondaga, Cayuga, Seneca, and Tuscarora. Together the tribes were known as the Iroquois.

American colonists observed that the members of the six Iroquois nations managed to have a stable and violence-free society without police or jails. They also appreciated that the people of the six tribes enjoyed free speech and carried out local decision making by using representative bodies called Grand Councils. These governmental principles would find their way into the U.S. Declaration of Independence and Constitution.

The Gayaneshakgowa—the Iroquois Great Law of Peace—is perhaps the most important tradition passed on by the Iroquois Confederacy. It was a system that helped tribes negotiate differences among themselves peacefully, guided by a wish for the common good. It also encouraged an orderly and nonviolent transfer of power from one leader to another. Finally, it instructed these leaders always to keep in mind their responsibilities to their descendants seven generations into the future.

According to legend, the founding nations of the Iroquois Confederacy were brought together by a Peacemaker, who bundled together some arrows and demonstrated how difficult it was to break them when they were joined, and how easy it was when they were separated. The Peacemaker also made the eagle a symbol of the vigilance required to spot conflicts among the tribes before these difficulties could become disruptive.

These symbols from the Iroquois Confederacy were eventually adopted by the United States. They can be seen on U.S. money and in many other places. It is interesting to note that Native Americans once referred to the members of the thirteen original American colonies as "the brothers of the thirteen fires," thus showing that they regarded their negotiating partners with sincere respect.

were given a voice in this international forum. It was a historic event.

"For forty years, the nations of the Iroquois Confederacy had been going to the UN and saying, 'What about us? We are people who have been colonized, but we are nations, too. And we need to have some forum.' That was the first time that that has ever happened," Winona explains. The Iroquois Confederacy was an early group of seven North American Indian tribes that made decisions together.

Jimmie Durham's group was one of those chosen to speak at the conference. As a research assistant, Winona was asked to gather information and prepare a document about the effects of uranium mining on the Navajo people. After she had completed it, she was invited to present it and give testimony about what she had learned through her research and through doing her own interviews.

Winona points out that when she gave her testimony before the UN, she was not making a speech about her own opinions, as she would years later. She was being entrusted to be the voice for many people she had interviewed, people who could not be present themselves. It was a role she undertook

Like many Navajo, Nellie Martin is a farmer who depends on the land for her living. She grazes her sheep on a reservation near Navajo, New Mexico, and spins the sheep's wool to weave into rugs. Here she bottle feeds a lamb on her farm.

What problems do Native peoples face today?

Almost all of the many serious problems faced by Native Americans today have a single origin—the disruption of traditional ways of life caused by the forced removal of people from their historic tribal lands. Pushed onto reservations, Native people are often cut off from the natural resources that allowed them to live by hunting, fishing, and the cultivation of staple crops.

Even where Native Americans remain on traditional lands, environmental pollution has made it difficult, impractical, or unhealthy to fish or hunt. The loss of the traditional ways of life has forced indigenous peoples to rely on making money and having jobs to provide themselves with what they need to live. However, jobs are scarce on reservations, and educational opportunities are limited. Per capita income is low.

Poverty creates a whole cluster of problems that tend to persist from generation to generation. Because of isolation and harsh conditions, alcoholism and substance abuse are widespread on reservations. Poverty also places great strains on families. Divorce is common on reservations, as is domestic violence and mental illness. As families are threatened, the fabric of community tends to come apart as well. This erosion of community threatens the survival of culture, language, and traditions.

The way to reverse these threats to Native American communities lies in local economic development. The influx of money from casinos has provided new financial wealth to some tribes. But ending poverty is not enough. A commitment to language, culture, crafts, and traditional ways of life is also necessary. Money alone will not solve the problems of Native American communities.

with a sense of both responsibility and humility.

Over the next few years, between 1978 and 1981, Winona continued her studies at Harvard. Economics was the subject she focused on, because she wanted to learn how to help Native American communities start businesses. She hoped to work in Native communities to overcome the poverty that prevented tribes from keeping control of their land and their lives.

During the summers she went to the Southwest, where she researched the effects of uranium mining on the health of people living on Navajo reservations.

She also worked on campaigns to protect the environment in several states. As a volunteer in such groups as the National Indian Youth Council and the New Mexico Indian Environmental Education Project, she was inspired by the dedication of committed activists. She learned a great deal from them about fighting political battles.

One of the things that Winona saw firsthand in the Southwest was that damage to the environment threatened not only the health of Native Americans but also the survival of their ways of life. The mining of uranium to make nuclear bombs and to fuel power plants was killing Navajo people and making their traditional lands unlivable. When they were forced to leave their land, Native people often lost their connection to their families, their history, and their culture.

Winona also saw how difficult it was for people on reservations to get information. If she wanted to find out what a mining corporation was doing to a reservation, it was much easier thousands of miles away in her college library, than when she was at the reservation itself.

After graduating from Harvard in 1982, Winona spent an extra year in a special college program studying how to build strong communities. When she finished, there were many doors that were open to her. She had distinguished herself both as a student and as a potential leader. Winona, however, had no doubt about which direction she would choose.

She had been brought up in a household where "doing the right thing" meant doing work that allowed you to use your best talents to help others.

Seeing the results of this work was the only kind of wealth that mattered to her. And so Winona was going where she was most needed. She was going to the White Earth reservation in Minnesota, the place her father came from and where many of his tribe, the Anishinaabeg, lived. She was going home.

Chapter 5
GIIWE—"COMING HOME"

As many of her Harvard classmates were beginning well-paying careers working for corporations and banks, Winona was setting out in another direction. Her path was rewarding, too, but the rewards came in a very different form.

Winona began her new life in a trailer on White Earth. "This is the land where I feel most comfortable in the world," she says today. It is certainly a beautiful place, but its specialness does not come just from its beauty. For Winona, White Earth is like nowhere else could be.

Her parents brought her to the reservation before she was old enough to talk, but she always remembered how it looked. When she came back, she had the sense that she was in a place she knew better than any other. "I clearly remembered my grandmother's house when I drove up to it in '81. I went to go find her farmhouse and I recognized it when I saw it."

But it wasn't just the houses that instantly told her she was home—it was the faces of the people. At a powwow, she looked across the arena as people were dancing and had a sudden insight. She realized that she was looking at the same people in the same community in which her ancestors had seen their relatives. She felt connected to something timeless and was sure at last that this was the place where she belonged.

The land at White Earth includes forest, marshes, and grassland, or prairie. In addition to hunting and fishing here, the Anishinaabeg traditionally used the plants and trees of the region for food and medicine and for making objects needed in daily life.

The Anishinaabeg had lived among the forests and lakes around White Earth for more than 30,000 years. Their close and respectful relationship to this land became the guiding basis of their way of life. In returning to this beautiful place, Winona was also renewing her connection to a timeless intergenerational community that she had always been a part of.

But White Earth was also a troubled place. The Anishinaabeg had lost ownership of all but a small amount of their land.

As a community, the reservation had one of the lowest levels of income anywhere in the United States. Eighty-five percent of its adults were unemployed. More than half of the Anishinaabeg students dropped out before finishing high school.

Other problems related to poverty also threatened White Earth, such as high levels of alcoholism, untreated mental illness, and violence within families. As the principal of the reservation high school, a job

Where is White Earth? What is its history?

The Anishinaabeg (who have also been called the Chippewa and Ojibwe by outsiders) are a Native American people who have lived in the area north of Lake Huron for thousands of years. With the arrival of Europeans, they migrated—and settled in the midwestern United States and Canada.

The White Earth reservation was created in 1867 as a homeland for the Anishinaabeg of northern Minnesota. They were allotted land that did not have mineral resources, but included prairie and ancient pine forests. The name "White Earth" comes from the color of the white clay found in much of the area. The land did not remain in the hands of Native people for very long. First, logging companies clear-cut nearly all the forests on the reservation. Then government officials and various businesspeople found ways to seize or cheaply buy the vast majority of White Earth. What had been 837,000 acres was down to 7,890 after about seventy years.

As the Anishinaabeg lost their forests, they also lost ways of living that had developed over thousands of years. They lost the birch trees they used to build canoes to harvest wild rice. And with the trees, they lost the materials they used to create baskets and the plants they used to make medicines.

Without these resources, many of the Anishinaabeg died. Between 1910 and 1920, epidemics sickened and killed much of the population. By 1930, fewer than 5,000 remained living on the reservation. Those who remained generally lived in poverty, crowded into houses on the small slice of land that was left to them.

Through the 1950s conditions were harsh on White Earth. The federal government's "help" came in the form of free, one-way bus tickets to the city. Many people saw no other choice but to leave. More than half of the enrolled members of the tribe went to live in cities off the reservation.

Today much of what was White Earth is held by vacationers with lakeside summer cottages, by farmers, and by the government. In recent years, however, the Anishinaabeg have begun to reverse their historic losses and begin to recover control of small but growing amounts of land.

White Earth is located in northwestern Minnesota. Only about 10 percent of the land on the reservation is owned by the Anishinaabeg. The rest of the land has become the property of the U.S. government and private non-Indian owners.

she began in 1982, Winona saw firsthand how terribly these problems were ravaging the community.

Winona recognized that these problems had a common source. Beginning with the first European settlers and continuing through the twentieth century, government, businesses, and individuals had taken ownership of much of White Earth away from the Anishinaabeg. Without the land, the tribe was like a plant taken from its soil.

Winona wanted to help restore the health of her people, their culture, and the community by working to get this land back. To do this, she left her position with the high school after a year, and helped organize a legal fight against the government to try to recover the land that it and others had taken unfairly and illegally from the Anishinaabeg.

It was a fight that would take years. Between 1982 and 1989, Winona worked with groups that used every possible legal method to try to get the land returned. They went to court in their own state of Minnesota, and they went to Washington, D.C., to appeal to the U.S. Congress and the Supreme Court. In the end, all these avenues ended in failure. The courts only returned a tiny percentage of the lost land. They ruled that the land had been taken illegally, but that too much time had gone by to give it back.

As difficult and complicated as the White Earth legal struggles were, they were only a part of what occupied Winona's time. She was an activist, a person who works to call problems to the attention of government officials or the public.

Often activists work to make small but important changes in their local communities, such as stopping pollution in a neighborhood. Sometimes they work on much larger issues, such as stopping the harm caused by wars or poverty. Winona's work on local problems at White Earth led her to work on national and international problems as well.

Groups such as the Native American Youth Council brought Winona together with people from different tribes. She became aware that similar kinds of struggles for land and survival were going on in Native communities throughout the United States and Canada and beyond.

From her home base of White Earth, Winona traveled frequently throughout the 1980s to assist other activists in their local struggles and to attend conferences. She found that at the head of these efforts to restore community health, there were often strong women, providing leadership and energy.

Winona interviews Rosalie Little Thunder, one of the founders of Buffalo Nations, an activist group that works to preserve the buffalo of the Great Plains. As a resident of Rosebud reservation in South Dakota, Rosalie became aware of the buffalo's importance both to the ecosystem of the plains and to the spiritual life of the Lakota Sioux, her tribe.

This was not just coincidence. In many Native societies women have traditionally held positions of responsibility and authority. These roles evolved naturally from their role as mothers—givers and nurturers of life.

Winona discovered that indigenous women were now facing many difficult issues of survival. Their societies were being disrupted and their lands destroyed. Some of the most severe concentrations of nuclear waste, chemical pollution, and other hazards were found on the lands of indigenous people. Nearly all atomic bomb tests in the United States had occurred on their lands or in their waters. The women recognized the effects of this pollution because poisons started to show up in their own bodies.

Winona researched this problem. She found that industrial chemicals like dioxin and PCBs (polychlorinated biphenyls) were accumulating in the water and soil on Native lands. The chemicals contaminated the breast milk of mothers who drank the water. Then the milk contaminated their children. Pollution affects people everywhere, but because governments had allowed it to be even more severe in Native areas, the problems were worse there. Because of water and fish contamination, for example, Inuit women who live in the Hudson Bay region of the Arctic were found to have the highest levels of breast milk contamination in the world. The frequency of breast cancer among the Inuit had grown as well.

Winona also learned that indigenous women were more than four times as likely as other women to be

How does pollution affect an entire ecosystem?

Because of the interdependence of living things, pollution of air, water, or soil can have a catastrophic effect on an entire ecosystem. An ecosystem is a set of delicate balances that maintains the natural environment both at the local level and on a global scale.

When a town dumps sewage or a factory dumps chemicals in a river, it is not just the fish that are affected. Birds and larger animals like bears, which eat fish or depend on the river as a drinking source, absorb some of the toxic chemicals. Reptiles that feed on insects also may become more scarce, thus allowing insect populations to grow and damage trees and plants.

Sometimes pollution spreads across several ecosystems and contributes to global environmental change. For example, air pollution from cars and the burning of fossil

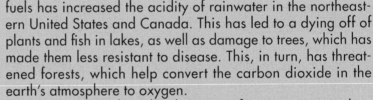

fuels has increased the acidity of rainwater in the northeastern United States and Canada. This has led to a dying off of plants and fish in lakes, as well as damage to trees, which has made them less resistant to disease. This, in turn, has threatened forests, which help convert the carbon dioxide in the earth's atmosphere to oxygen.

Scientists speculate that because of increases in carbon dioxide, the entire planet is gradually warming. This warming is already bringing with it harmful and unusual storms, droughts, and extended rain and flooding.

In the case of acid rain, the smoke from power plants and cars in the Northeast travels hundreds of miles to damage the environments of distant lakes. The harmful effects of pollution are not just limited to the area where it occurs.

Acid rain, which results from the burning of coal, oil, and other fossil fuels, can cause severe damage to trees. When trees die from acid rain, as these have, insects, animals, and plants throughout an ecosystem are affected.

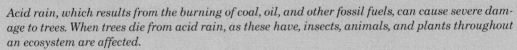

hurt by someone in their families. Widespread poverty in indigenous communities leads to many social problems, including alcoholism and violence against women by men.

To aid each other in confronting these issues, Janet McCloud, Ingrid Washinawatok El Issa,

At a meeting in 1989, Winona (holding daughter Waseyabin) and other members of the IWN wear traditional Hawai'ian leis and wreaths. The IWN brings together indigenous women from North America and many other parts of the world.

Winona, and five other activists formed the Indigenous Women's Network (IWN) in 1985. Although the members lived and worked thousands of miles away from each other, they held yearly gatherings where more than four hundred activist women would meet to explore collective solutions to their shared concerns. These included fighting poverty and social problems, protecting the environment and health of their people, recovering tribal land, and preserving and keeping alive vanishing tribal languages and cultures.

As the IWN grew, it supported local projects that helped women become leaders in their communities. These projects sometimes began with small actions. For example, the IWN helped support a diaper service on the Cree reservation, at Moose Factory, in James Bay, Canada. This service allowed working mothers who couldn't afford washing machines to stop buying disposable diapers. Not only did this save money for the mothers, but it also helped reduce the environmental damage caused by the production and disposal of plastic diapers.

This was a small victory, and one that Winona helped to organize. In time she and other IWN activists would enjoy a very large victory as well. But first Winona would focus on her family and her home at White Earth. At a conference in Toronto in 1986, she met and befriended another activist, Randy Kapashesit, a political representative of the Cree tribe from Moose Factory in Canada.

Two years after she and Randy met, they married. In that same year, 1988, their first child was born. She was named Waseyabin ("Light of Day") and would later go by the nickname of "Wasey." Their second child, a boy named Ajuawak ("Crossing the

By 1990 Winona's family included her new son, Ajuawak, whom she holds on her lap here, in addition to her daughter, Waseyabin, and husband, Randy.

Water") was born in 1990. The new family lived in Moose Factory, but Winona maintained her ties to White Earth as well.

In the meantime Winona's work with the IWN had begun to attract attention. In 1989 she received the Reebok Human Rights Award, a recognition for activists younger than thirty years of age. The award came with a prize of $20,000. She used this money to establish the White Earth Land Recovery Project (WELRP), a nonprofit organization dedicated to reversing the Anishinaabeg's loss of land. Winona wanted to heal her community and protect its environment and traditional culture.

With the WELRP, Winona could explore new ways to get land transferred back from the U.S. government to the White Earth tribal government. Since the legal courts had not been helpful in the past, the WELRP welcomed and encouraged gifts of money to purchase land, or outright gifts of land itself. As of 2000, the WELRP had bought more than 1,400 acres to keep them from being cleared, built on, or turned into large farms or housing developments.

Most of this land is maple sugarbush, where sap is collected from trees to be boiled and made into syrup. One of Winona's goals in starting the WELRP was to support traditional kinds of harvesting and agriculture. The use of traditional farming methods has enabled people living on White Earth to earn an income without damaging the land. As syrup harvester Ron Chilton explains, "You can cut a tree down once and get some money, but if you make syrup every year, you will get money, you will get food, a sweet taste, you will smell spring, and you will get food for your soul."

What is sustainable development?

The manufacture of a single automobile produces an enormous amount of pollution. Each time a car is made, the earth is damaged by the disposal of toxic waste, the burning of fuel, the mining of steel, and other processes that pollute air, rivers, and the ground.

Fortunately for the earth, not everyone is destined to own a car. Most people around the world can't afford them, but if they could, the environmental damage that six billion automobiles would cause would make the earth uninhabitable.

Sustainable development is economic growth that takes into account the environmental effects of commercial activity. Though sustaining the environment seems like a good idea to many individuals, it is less popular with corporations. Because of the pressure on businesses to show short-term, immediate profits, sustainable development is often ignored in favor of large-scale, environmentally destructive ways of making money. These include cutting down forests to make paper or destroying natural fisheries by dragging huge nets from giant fishing boats.

Examples of sustainable development include selective harvesting of trees, using farming practices that put nutrients back into the soil, and developing low-cost sources of wind, water, or solar energy. It is possible to make a profit while practicing sustainable development. What this requires is the ability to plan for the future and sacrifice immediate profit for long-term survival.

There have been other harvesting activities at White Earth as well. On the land near its office, the WELRP maintains a mill for processing wild rice harvested by local gatherers. It has also established fields of raspberry and strawberry plants. In 1999 these fields produced more than 2,700 pints of fruit for sale as jam and produce. The WELRP has also helped grow traditional hominy corn to provide food for local tribal elders and youth programs.

Some modern technology has been added to traditional agriculture at White Earth, but with a conscious effort to use techniques that do minimal environmental damage. Instead of propane or gas fuel, old-fashioned wood fires are used to cook the maple syrup. Unlike the other fuels, wood is a local source of energy that gets replaced as the forest grows. Instead of running pollution-spewing diesel trucks, farmers at White Earth use horses to power carts for transportation, plowing, and harvesting.

The WELRP has sponsored other projects that combine European and Anishinaabeg technology in ways that protect the environment while allowing people to make a living on the land. One example is a project that explores how to harvest timber in a way that allows the forests to stay healthy. This balance has already been accomplished on the Menominee reservation in Wisconsin. Forests there have the same number of trees as they did 150 years ago, but the Menominee have a very successful forest-products industry.

Along with its efforts to support a traditional way of life that doesn't use up the land or damage the environment, the WELRP has also put a strong emphasis on preserving culture through education.

This has been very important because modern life is rapidly eroding traditional customs, such as hunting and drumming, and even the traditional language. According to Robynn Carter, WELRP community organizer, "There has been an eighty percent language loss on the reservation recently. There's only about thirty elders that speak Ojibwe."

The WELRP started a language program for preschoolers so children could learn basic Ojibwe vocabulary and begin to build sentences and sing songs. It helped sponsor language classes for teenagers and

Wild rice is harvested from the lakes at White Earth each fall. Anishinaabeg families go out in canoes pushed by pole. They bend the rice plants over the edge of the canoe and gently brush the grains onto its floor. Later the rice is spread to dry and then parched in large metal drums.

A visiting Native musician introduces students at a White Earth school to traditional Ojibwe music. Signs placed next to familiar objects help students learn new Ojibwe words.

adults as well. Instructor Robert Tibbetts explains that some of the traditional, tribal ways of understanding things can only be expressed in Ojibwe, and not in English. For example, Ojibwe does not make a sharp distinction between things that are alive and things named as objects. "In English, you say 'a drum' and that's not a living thing, but talk about a drum in Ojibwe and it's just like it's a person, and you recognize the spirit that's in that drum," he explains.

Many Anishinaabeg notice the effects of the WELRP efforts to restore culture. Winona's organization has set up programs for grade school students; camps for teenagers that teach the traditional outdoor survival skills of fishing, trapping, and tracking; summer activities for children featuring language and crafts; and sales of craft and artwork by local artists.

The WELRP points to a way the Anishinaabeg can recover their traditional way of life and thrive in the modern world. With a staff of fewer than ten people, including Winona, it has been able to accomplish significant things at White Earth.

For Winona, the impulse to help create and sustain a community is as consuming as her work in raising her young children, playing with them, reading to them, and helping them learn to be responsible for themselves and each other. Through the exercise of many talents and with much spirit and imagination, Winona has found a way to be an activist and a mother at the same time. She offered an explanation for how she accomplishes this when a reporter for the girl's magazine *New Moon* asked her to describe her greatest passion: "I suppose you could say I like to grow things," Winona said. "I don't mean my garden, which is usually kind of weedy. I like to grow projects. I like to see something start from an idea and become something."

Chapter 6

HONORING THE EARTH

Winona's work as an activist took her not just beyond her home, and not just beyond White Earth, but into the national and international arena. In 1991 she was named to the board of directors of Greenpeace, the worldwide environmental organization. Greenpeace is known for its educational work and its protests against the destruction of the environment wherever it occurs. Winona's participation on Greenpeace's board has helped bring the perspectives of indigenous people and women to the organization.

Greenpeace selected Winona because, in addition to speaking and writing about the environment, she was involved in one of the most important ongoing struggles to defend it. Winona was one of the many activists who opposed a project known as James Bay II. And her side eventually won.

The history of the James Bay project went back to the 1970s. At that time, a government power company in Canada planned to make a series of dams to change the flow of rivers in the north. Their plan was to use dammed and redirected water to make electric power that could be sold to consumers in the United States.

The first part of the project was called James Bay I, and it caused an environmental disaster. When land was flooded, mercury, a highly poisonous metal, got drawn out of the soil and into the water. The Cree people of the area, who depended on fish, were

During the first phase of the James Bay Hydroelectric Project, four smaller rivers were diverted into the La Grande River by means of dams and dikes, thus flooding many miles of forest and creating the La Grande Reservoir in Quebec. Dams at the edge of the reservoir, like this one, contain hydroelectric power plants, which generate electricity from the water pressure.

warned not to eat them any more. The floods of toxic water also killed numerous water-based creatures and more than ten thousand caribou in one year.

The second part of the project, James Bay II, was going to cost $60 billion, and it would have meant massive flooding of wildlife areas and the destruction of forests the size of Maine, Vermont, and New York State combined.

Winona and others who opposed James Bay II helped bring together many organizations with a common interest in stopping the project. She had a personal connection to this battle because this was the area where her husband had been born and still lived, and where the family spent much of the year. The groups that joined the struggle included the Cree and Innu people, the IWN, student groups, conservation and environmental groups, human rights groups, and even concerned electric power consumers in New York and in Vermont and other New England states.

This alliance of many people challenged the James Bay project in different ways. Students persuaded their schools to take back school money invested in the power company. The Native community complained to the government bureaus that consider what's fair for power companies to do. Others went to speak at the meetings of the directors of the power company.

All these efforts added up to a winning result. By 1996, after enduring more than six years of determined battle from activists, the Canadian power company that planned James Bay II finally abandoned its plans for the project. This was a historic victory that demonstrated the power of activists and organizations unafraid to take a stand together and fight with persistence and patience against a powerful opponent.

As her involvement in the James Bay struggle demonstrates, being a mother has never slowed down Winona's ability to do things in the world. In fact, motherhood seems to have served as a jump start for some of her most ambitious projects.

For example, in 1988, the same year that Waseyabin was born, Winona established the WELRP and finished graduate school, earning a master's degree in rural development from Antioch University. Two years later, when she was pregnant with her son Ajuawak, she began what would be seven years of work on a novel.

"I credit that book to my son," Winona explains. "It must have been him because I'm not by and large a fiction writer." As part of her work as an activist, she had written studies about social and environmental

Winona speaks to a television reporter at White Earth about Native American land recovery and environmental concerns. It is her job, as director of the WELRP, to explain the project's activities to people both on and off the reservation.

problems that were used by organizations or published in newspapers and magazines. Fiction is a very different kind of writing, but she was also good at it. Her widely praised novel, *Last Standing Woman,* was eventually published in 1997.

In her years at White Earth and in many other indigenous communities, Winona had heard life stories and tribal histories from hundreds of people. Although she used some of this information in her writing for newspapers and magazines, much of it was never written down. The faces of those she had talked to and their stories would come back to her at night. "I started developing writer's insomnia," she says.

She decided to record what she remembered in order to preserve the history of her people. She wove together stories based on what she had heard or witnessed, and as she added to them, her book eventually became a novel spanning seven generations. The events described start in 1800 and stretch into the future, ending with a hopeful vision of the Anishinaabeg community in the twenty-first century.

In the book's later chapters, a fictional character named Alanis Nordstrom appears, who in many ways (but not all) resembles Winona herself. Like Winona, Alanis is a journalist. Unlike Winona, she has to decide whether or not to stay with her ancestral community or try to be successful in the non-Indian world. Winona is clear that this was never her personal struggle. She never sought success that required her to leave her community behind. Still, Winona notes, this is a common situation. Native Americans often find that opportunities for success require them to abandon their communities and her-

Despite her many responsibilities outside the home, Winona has always placed a priority on her role as a mother. Here she and Waseyabin stand in front of a painting by Betty LaDuke.

itage. Winona patterned Alanis after a number of women whom she knew or grew up with.

Though she did not face this dilemma, she did face another that stemmed from her bond to her community. Winona knew her life had to be at White Earth, but her husband, Randy, was just as linked to his community in Moose Factory, twenty-six hours away by car and train.

"I couldn't give up my life, because in a little while I'd be angry," Winona states, explaining why she wouldn't move to Moose Factory. Instead, she and her husband agreed to separate in 1992. "He's one of my best friends still," she said recently. Their separation meant that she would take on a difficult new role—that of a single, working mother.

Winona acknowledges that keeping a balance between her various responsibilities was a challenge. However, it helped her that she was living in a place where people of all ages knew and supported each other, where adults and older children could be counted on to look after the community's children at times. Winona also saw her activist work as part of her job as a mother to make a better place for everyone's children—including her own—to grow up in.

During the James Bay years, Winona participated in many other fights to protect the environment. Sometimes this work involved putting herself at personal risk. In September 1994, she took part in an act of civil disobedience outside a phone book factory in Los Angeles. People from Clayquot Sound, Canada, asked Winona if she would join their protest. They accused the phone company GTE (General Telephone) of using wood that had been clear-cut from their

What is civil disobedience?

Throughout history, people have stood up to injustice by refusing to cooperate with unfair laws and government policies. In the twentieth century, civil disobedience brought about major political changes in some countries, by forcing government to respect public opinion.

One of the most powerful examples of this occurred in 1930, when Mohandas Gandhi helped organize a protest against one of the laws that made life hard for the people of India. At that time, Britain ruled India and prevented Indians from manufacturing and selling salt.

Instead of organizing a violent uprising, Gandhi organized a two-hundred-mile march. People joined this march as it went through villages, and as their numbers grew, they attracted more and more attention. The British jailed 100,000 marchers, but this was not enough to stop Gandhi's nonviolent movement. Eventually Britain was forced to give up its control of India.

Some examples of civil disobedience in the United States include sit-down strikes in auto plants during the 1930s, the Montgomery bus boycott of the 1950s, and the marches for civil rights and protests against the Vietnam War in the 1960s.

More recently, nonviolent demonstrations at meetings of the World Trade Organization, the International Monetary Fund, and the Democratic and Republican political conventions brought attention to the fact that these organizations were making decisions without input from most American citizens.

The power of civil disobedience comes from the courage of individuals who are willing to face personal risk of arrest and violence without threatening other people. History has shown that the willingness of people to organize and speak out together for justice is difficult for even the most powerful government to resist.

Protesters block a downtown Seattle street in an act of civil disobedience during the 1999 demonstrations against the World Trade Organization. Its opponents see the organization, which promotes global trade, as helping big corporations exploit poor workers and natural resources in the Third World, often with harmful consequences for the environment.

forests, including new trees and others that were more than a thousand years old.

"I don't think a thousand-year-old tree should be made into a phone book. I spent most of my life living in forests. And I love those trees," Winona explained.

Her certainty that cutting down the trees was wrong ran very strongly in her, so much so that she was willing to be arrested. Five other activists were with her. They chained themselves to the gates of the factory to prevent trucks from passing through and the guards from removing them.

They stood there in the hot sun for many hours. Eventually, the police arrived with helmets and shields. There were more than thirty of them. They began marching around like soldiers, as if they were about to attack the protesters.

Winona recalls her reaction: "Holy buckets!" She knew that she had to stay where she was.

The police cut the protesters' chains and arrested them. They were taken to the Los Angeles County Jail and held for four hours. It was the only time that Winona had been arrested, but she saw it as another part of the same work that she had always been doing.

"I'm someone who's litigated in court and gone to Congress, been to administrative hearing processes and worked on civil disobedience and demonstrated before—so getting arrested was a continuation of the same work," she says. Activists, like house builders, use a variety of tools. One situation may call for the hammer of protest, and another may require a tool that is more precise and subtle.

Winona discovered a powerful new way to work for positive change when she met the Indigo Girls. Musicians Amy Ray and Emily Saliers from Atlanta,

Georgia, headed a very well-known and successful band for more than ten years. Their music has been called "progressive folk/rock," but it is really in its own category. Amy and Emily's voices blend in an unexpected way, and the two singers have "a sort of sisterlike relationship," according to Emily.

Over the years, Emily and Amy had made a practice of donating their time and money to promote causes that they believed in. Some of these causes included environmental protection, women's health and reproductive choice, defense of indigenous lands, and housing for the homeless.

Winona saw the Indigo Girls in action in New York City in 1991, when she went to a benefit concert that they did on behalf of the effort to stop James Bay II. Amy and Emily talked about how they were interested in doing other benefit concerts. Together the three women came up with the idea of doing a concert tour that would both raise money for indigenous

Winona and the Indigo Girls (Emily Saliers, left, and Amy Ray, right) organized the Honor the Earth tours to draw attention to environmental problems and to raise money for indigenous groups.

groups and publicize environmental damage that needed to be stopped.

This willingness to take a principled stand at the risk of losing popularity with fans or record companies made the Indigo Girls unusual among pop stars. Most stars do not like to talk about controversial subjects, but the Indigo Girls won over many fans because of the independence and truthfulness that they show both in their music and in their lives. They are popular because they seem comfortable with who they are and aren't afraid to be different or have opinions.

While the Indigo Girls have learned a lot from Winona about being activists, she has learned a lot from them as well. "The Girls have been a significant influence on me because they are really human. . . . They are these incredibly compassionate, interesting, amusing women who happen to be gifted musicians. And I consider them first as friends, and then as musicians," she says.

In 1993 the Indigo Girls did a three-city tour to benefit the IWN. Winona spoke at each concert. They also performed at a benefit concert in Quebec called the "Ban the Dam Jam" to raise awareness and money for the fight to stop the James Bay II project. This short tour would prove to be a test run for a much more ambitious series of benefit concerts in May and June 1995.

That twenty-one-concert series was called the "Honor the Earth 1995" tour. During each concert, usually midway through, activists would inform the audience about specific problems affecting Native Americans, such as the slaughter of buffalo in South Dakota and the dumping of nuclear waste in Nevada.

They discussed ways the public could help stop these things and make positive changes in the world. In each city, local activists were invited to speak, in addition to Winona and others.

After listening to the speakers, concertgoers were invited to sign action cards. These postcards allowed people to register their opinions and urge public officials to take a particular action on an issue. One example of such a card was addressed to the secretary of the interior, requesting that the National Park Service stop its policy of slaughtering wild buffalo when the buffalo left the borders of a park.

The results of the 1995 tour were impressive. It was a kind of a national teach-in with more than 50,000 participants. It generated more than $250,000 dollars in donations, which were used by forty-one local campaigns around the country to stop pollution or help Native people. For many of these locally based groups, even a modest amount of money could go a long way. Some believe that the tour was the largest single fund-raising event in the history of Native American activism.

In addition, the tour provided an opportunity to get coverage in the news for the issues that the Indigo Girls and Winona cared about. Environmental problems and Native American concerns were usually ignored by newspapers and TV news shows.

"And it's not that Indians are silent on these issues," Winona declared. Winona herself had spoken out and had been heard. In 1994 *Time* magazine named her as one of "America's most promising leaders age forty and under." She felt strongly, though, that a great many people with important information were being overlooked. The reason for this lack of attention to local people's views is that most newspapers and TV shows depend on the support of government and large corporations. This affects what they can say and prevents them from criticizing government and big business.

Winona, Amy, and Emily realized that the media attention that the Indigo Girls attracted was an opportunity to bring important information and ideas to people. "We reach people who would probably never hear our voices but who come to an Indigo Girls show. They come up to me afterward and they say, 'I never really thought about that issue. Thank you for saying that.' And maybe you gave them the idea that they can make a difference," Winona reflected.

The success of the 1995 tour led to another in 1997. The common theme of this second tour was the need to stop the Nuclear Waste Policy Act, which was being considered in Congress. This act proposed the creation of a national dump for high-level nuclear waste on the sacred lands of the western Shoshone people in Nevada. Ninety thousand shipments of extremely dangerous material would be carried to the dump by trucks through inhabited areas. Even an ordinary traffic accident with one of these trucks would have catastrophic consequences. Winona pointed out that more than 50 million people lived within a half mile of the highways the trucks would use. On the 1997 concert tour, more than 15,000 people signed cards asking President Clinton to veto this bill.

Signed cards also had a significant impact in reversing the industrial pollution of the St. Lawrence River. For years, Mohawk activist and midwife Katsi Cook had been trying to get a meeting with the head of the

Why is pollution "environmental racism"?

Most people agree that where people live in the United States is strongly affected by race and ethnicity. Racial and immigrant groups may voluntarily cluster in areas where there are neighbors, houses of worship, and merchants who share their culture.

However, this grouping by race may also be determined by involuntary factors such as job or housing discrimination. Although such discrimination is technically illegal, the cost of housing serves as an informal but effective barrier to racial and ethnic groups with historically low incomes. For this reason, it is predictable which groups live in which areas.

The effects of environmental pollution can often be concentrated in a particular location. For example, the placement of a factory or garbage incinerator can result in increased illnesses in that area. In southeast Chicago, in East St. Louis, in Louisiana's "Cancer Alley," and on Navajo lands where uranium is mined, the linkage of racial grouping, poverty and environmental pollution is distinct. Native Americans, in particular, have suffered a heavy burden of localized environmental pollution. One reason for this is that their communities are often located far from where wealthy or politically powerful people live.

This lack of clout can put Native Americans on the unfair side of things when a political decision has to be made about where to locate a dam, a mine, a dump, a military base, or a bombing range.

While environmental racism is unjust, there are ways to combat it. One way is for communities to organize and unite to oppose damaging projects planned for their areas. Another is for people to organize across racial and ethnic lines to find a common cause in opposing destruction of the environment and threats to public health wherever they occur.

Environmental Protection Agency to call attention to some severe health hazards in her community. Her Akwesasne Mohawk reservation was identified as the most polluted in the Great Lakes region near the St. Lawrence.

For ten years, representatives of the agency refused to meet with her. In 1997, after Katsi spoke on the Honor the Earth tour, Carol Browner, the director of the Environmental Protection Agency, agreed to a meeting. Secretary Browner had received more than 3,500 signed cards on the issue of the urgency of Akwesasne cleanup from people who had attended the concerts.

Concert tours could be a powerful tool, but Winona recognized their limits as well. She was pleased that people were learning about the environment and the problems of Native peoples. And yet not everyone in the audience was moved to take action. Still, everyone was at least able to hear a new message. Perhaps it was the beginning of a new awareness for many people.

The Indigo Girls and the Honor the Earth organization did another tour in 2000. Spanning eight states, the tour included appearances by the artists Bonnie Raitt, Joan Baez, and Jackson Browne, three performers with a long history of actively and visibly supporting progressive causes. It also included Indigenous and Annie Humphrey, Native performers who are very popular in Indian communities. The concerts helped register several thousand voters.

Winona's life had extended outward in wide circles. In the center of the circle was her own household and children. Then came the circle of her community at White Earth. Beyond that was the circle of Native and indigenous communities. This circle extended around the world.

In August 1995, Winona had the chance to share her experiences with women from many countries. She headed a delegation of representatives of the IWN to the UN World Conference on Women in Beijing, China.

From the steps of the Lincoln Memorial in Washington, D.C., Winona addresses a crowd gathered to celebrate Earth Day 2000. (The Washington Monument is visible in the background.) Earth Day was established as an annual event to honor the earth and confirm commitment to environmental goals, such as reducing carbon dioxide pollution from fossil fuels, saving the world's tropical rainforests, cleaning up nuclear waste sites to acceptable levels of safety, and increasing recycling programs in local communities.

Like the UN conference she had attended almost twenty years earlier, the Beijing conference was a forum for information and perspectives that had not generally been heard—in this case the perspectives of women. When ideas are shared in this way, it changes the way people think. This, in turn, can reshape the way they and their governments act.

Winona gave a speech titled "The Indigenous Women's Network: Our Future, Our Responsibility." In it, she said that the problems facing indigenous women were a more severe and harsh version of those facing all women and all of society. Rapid changes in technology and industry all over the world were putting women and societies further and further away from nature and undermining our ability to live in harmony with the earth.

She pointed out that there were 500 million indigenous people in the world. They did not have a voice in the UN, because indigenous people are not recognized under international law as nations. Corporations, however, such as oil, telephone, and mining companies, have rights that are even more powerful than those of nations.

"What law gives that right to them?" she asked the delegates. She then detailed some of the many ways that indigenous people were suffering from the actions of corporations. Winona reminded her listeners that when the environment is damaged, the risks to indigenous women are no worse than those to women, men, or children anywhere. We are all in the same boat.

"What befalls our mother Earth, befalls her daughter. . . . Simply stated, if we can no longer nurse our children, if we can no longer bear children, and if our bodies themselves are wracked with poisons, we will have accomplished little," she said.

She concluded by listing what the IWN believed are the basic rights and conditions that are necessary for a more just world. The first was that women deserve running water, basic housing, and health care, and that it was possible to attain these things without damaging the environment. Another was that indigenous peoples deserve recognition as nations, so that they can have a voice in issues that affect their health and survival.

By raising these points in an international forum, Winona was bringing a message to the global level where decisions were being made. The ideas she spoke about were not simply hers, but those of people who might never otherwise be heard. She felt a responsibility to represent these people, who would never have a chance to speak before the UN or any other governmental body.

Winona was someone who was increasingly spending her life speaking and writing in hopes of bringing an alternative vision into the world. Soon she would be offered yet another way to share her ideas about transforming society.

Chapter 7

A MOTHER'S ENERGY

There was a time when the health of the earth could not be put in danger by human beings. In recent years, new developments in science, technology, and industry have made humans more powerful. The earth is now affected by man-made chemicals, the use of atomic weapons and energy, and a rapidly growing human population already numbering in the billions. Weather has changed, some regions have been contaminated by pollution, and certain plants and animals have become extinct.

In the past few decades, a growing number of people around the world have started to question the direction that the United States and other wealthy nations have been taking. It seemed to them that governments needed to make their decisions with a greater regard for the well-being of the earth. This perspective, which indigenous peoples have always held sacred, was beginning to be shared by people all over the world.

In the early 1980s, a new international political movement started. The pro-environment, anti-nuclear Green Party got its start in Germany. Its candidates began to win seats in the German parliament, and the Greens' ideas spread. By 2000, there were active Green Parties in eighty countries. There were elected officials from the Green Party holding office

What is the Green Party?

The first "Greens" were people who were interested in peace, ecological balance, local democracy, and feminism.

Their movement began in Europe in reaction to plans to bring an especially dangerous kind of nuclear missile into Germany. Millions of Germans protested in the streets. As a result, the German Green Party was successful in getting representatives elected to the national parliament, or Bundestag.

From Germany, Green Party ideas spread to other countries. In the United States, the Green Party took part in national elections in 1996 and 2000, and it plans to run candidates in local elections in the future.

Through electoral politics, the Greens hope to transform life in industrialized societies according to ten key values:
1) Sensitivity to ecological balance
2) Opposition to poverty, to injustice, and to discrimination based on gender, race, and other factors.
3) Grassroots democracy—guaranteeing all citizens a direct voice in the decisions that affect their lives
4) Nonviolence
5) Decentralization of power and responsibility
6) Community economics
7) Feminism
8) Respect for diversity
9) Personal and global responsibility
10) Focus on the future—considering the impact of decisions on generations to come

The long-term strategy of the Green Party is to bring together electoral politics with local activism. It hopes to address the problems that have come from old ways of thinking, based on big business and a large military, with alternatives based on creating new institutions at the local level.

in several European countries, including Germany, France, Denmark, and Great Britain.

The Green Party in the United States was founded more recently, in 1984, but has grown steadily. By 1996 it was ready to run a national campaign. Its first candidate for president of the United States was

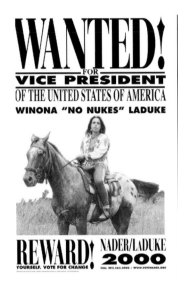

This poster was designed by Winona's friends for her 1996 campaign and reused in 2000. The knickname "No Nukes" refers to Winona's long-standing opposition to the development of nuclear power and nuclear weapons.

the highly respected public citizen and activist Ralph Nader. Its vice presidential candidate was Winona LaDuke.

Running for elective office had not been Winona's ambition. When Ralph Nader approached her to ask if she would agree to accept the nomination, she was honored, but not immediately sure it was what she should do. There was a lot to think about.

It is demanding and takes responsibility even to be a candidate for national office. At this level a candidate must try to be an advocate for the hopes of everyone affected by the decisions of the U.S. government.

Anyone running for such an important office has to be knowledgeable in many areas and learn about many more. Winona was a trained economist. She had studied at university how to use the tools of money, business, and investment to eliminate poverty. She had also studied the science of ecology, which explores the connections between living things and their environment. And she was very familiar with Native American teachings about the earth and its living creatures.

For Winona, all this knowledge, drawn from many sources, led to strong political beliefs. As she states in her book *All Our Relations*, "The rights of the people to use and enjoy air, water, and sunlight are essential to life, liberty, and the pursuit of happiness. These basic human rights have been impaired by those who discharge toxic substances into the air, water, and land. Contaminating the commons must be recognized as a fundamental wrong in our system of laws, just as defacing private property is wrong."

Still, there were real reasons for Winona to think carefully about running for vice president. She already had two jobs, as program director of both the WELRP and Honor the Earth. She also had two children and a household that included animals. It would be a challenge to add the enormous workload and travel of a national political campaign to a life that was already so full.

The reasons for accepting the challenge were compelling as well. She was dissatisfied with the policies of the federal government. Her upbringing had taught her that when something is wrong, a person has a responsibility to take action. Refusing this opportunity just because it was so challenging felt irresponsible to her.

Another reason was the enormous respect she had for Ralph Nader. Because of his work, cars have seatbelts and the United States has the Clean Air Act and the Freedom of Information Act, laws that dramatically improved air quality and allowed citi-

Winona and Ralph Nader speak at a Green Party campaign stop in 2000. Longtime activist Nader wanted Winona as his political running-mate because of her willingness to fight for what she believes in, her abilities as an organizer, and her gifts as a public speaker.

zens to learn more about the actions of government, so that the public could better judge if these actions were legal and fair. These are only some of his many contributions. Few activists have had a more positive impact on the lives of ordinary citizens than he has had.

Winona thought about this decision quite a lot. She asked for guidance from elders in her spiritual community and spoke to colleagues and friends she trusted. There were many people she had known and stood side by side with in the struggle to get justice for Native peoples. She felt a responsibility to try to do something that would help their cause.

Yet Winona realized that there were many others who were qualified to be the Green Party's vice presidential candidate. Before she could accept, she told the party, she would prefer to be considered among others. Ralph Nader agreed to put her name on a list of seven potential candidates. Soon after, he called back and said that both he and the Green Party were sure that she was the best candidate for the job.

"She's a rather remarkable person," Nader said, "in the sense that she's a leader on major issues involving indigenous people, environmental issues, and democracy. At the same time, she's running a household, a farm, a sugar bush, and dealing with issues close at hand. She goes right from the grassroots to the general policy levels of issues of justice and injustice."

Winona agreed to be the candidate. As a campaigner, she had numerous strengths. Her skills in debate and writing helped her communicate the Green Party's ideas well. She could answer challenging questions with ease and persuasiveness. More important, she

What is a grassroots movement?

Even in democracies, where political leaders are chosen by election, government does not always reflect the wishes of the people. Once elected, some leaders loose touch with what people want at the local level. In other cases, government officials pay more attention to big businesses or to wealthy individuals than to average voters.

Grassroots movements occur when people act independently of the interests of large organizations to take back control of issues that affect their lives. The meaning of the term "grassroots" comes from the way that grass sends out countless tiny roots that grip the soil. While other plants are relatively easy to pull out of the ground, the many, tiny roots of the grass plant make it much harder to remove.

In grassroots movements, people talk to their neighbors, hold meetings in their homes or places of worship, and try to influence politics personally. They don't wait for a national leader to bring issues up, they organize petitions, write to public officials, write letters to the editors of newspapers, and take part in marches or protests.

Often, a local issue might serve as the basis for a grassroots political action. The fight for civil rights in the 1960s involved grassroots local action, starting where abuses were worst. Environmental protests also tend to address local problems. Grassroots movements build slowly, but when they reach the national level, they can be strong and usually result in important changes.

had a passionate conviction about the message she was sharing, and her passion made others eager to support the issues she spoke about.

In theory, any political party can win an election in the United States. In fact, the two most wealthy parties, the Republicans and the Democrats, have large advantages that make it much more challenging for candidates outside those parties to get on the ballot and get their message out to voters.

Even so, candidates who were not Democrats or Republicans have often been able to introduce ideas that were too important or too popular to ignore. For example, so-called third parties called for the end of slavery and for women's right to vote well before

Democrats or Republicans were willing to raise these issues. Even when third-party candidates got only a small percentage of the vote, their campaigns changed history.

Supporters of the Green Party believed that international corporations had too much power. These corporations even controlled the U.S. government through giving money to politicians. There had to be new laws that would make the corporations accountable for harm that they were doing to the earth and to many citizens.

The Green Party's 1996 campaign fought for laws limiting the power of corporations. Some of the party's other goals were promoting clean sources of energy; guaranteeing health care for all citizens, regardless of their ability to pay; changing the way that political campaigns are paid for; and reducing the use of the military to resolve conflicts.

As she campaigned, Winona showed how her beliefs as a member of an indigenous society would translate into a new direction for the United States. One example was her promotion of a "Seventh Generation" amendment to the U.S. Constitution.

This amendment would reflect one of the teachings of the Six Nations Iroquois Confederacy: "In each deliberation, we must consider the impact on the seventh generation from now." Winona pointed out how following this idea would rule out the use of uranium, because nuclear waste threatens the future of our descendants for more than 100,000 years into the future.

In 1996 the Green Party was able to get on the ballot in twenty-one states. Across the country, the Nader-LaDuke ticket drew 684,902 votes—not enough to win office, but enough to establish the Greens on a national level.

After the elections, Winona continued, as always, to carry out important responsibilities on many levels. On the local level, the WELRP was starting new education programs at White Earth. At the national level, Winona continued to work with Honor the Earth, and at the international level she remained involved with the IWN. She was also at work revising the manuscript of her novel, *Last Standing Woman*.

When the novel was published, it was praised by many people. Reviewers called it a powerful and impressive work because of the skillful way that it brought together lively characters and accurate historical facts.

Following the publication of this novel, Winona wrote her first work of nonfiction. Published in 1999, it was titled *All Our Relations: Native Struggles for Land and Life*. The book documents the ways that various indigenous communities have responded to environmental and political challenges. At the same time, it documents Winona's own work as an activist over a twenty-year period. "That's pretty much the story of my life right there," she says of the book.

In it she describes how the Akwesasne Mohawk people sought a cleanup of their contaminated water and land. Another chapter explores how the Seminoles of Florida have responded to the erosion of their homeland in the Everglades due to overdevelopment and pollution. Other chapters describe how the ongoing slaughter of buffalo affects Native peoples in the Midwest, and how the U.S. occupation of Hawai'i affected the Native people of the islands. The book ends with a hopeful look at the way a Hopi electri-

Winona and Kevin Gasco stand outside a powwow in traditional dress.

cian is helping to bring alternative energy and self-sufficiency to the Hopi reservation where he lives.

During the period of writing and activism that followed the 1996 election, Winona met the man who would eventually become her second husband. Kevin Gasco had grown up in Ann Arbor, Michigan. Like Winona, he was the only Native American member of his high school class. He was also student body president.

Kevin was an enrolled member of the Traverse Bay band of Odawas in Michigan. He and Winona met at a Michigan powwow. Winona remembers that she was very visible at this particular event. She was one of the announcer-hosts, and she was dancing in a jingle dress—a form of traditional regalia.

Although he remained very involved in his own community, to which he returned regularly to take part in ceremonies, Kevin began to live with Winona at White Earth. She had a house on the reservation, near a lake. Originally a small cabin, it has grown as her family has. Kevin started a business selling coffee produced by natural farming practices. He and Winona would eventually have a child together, a boy named Gwekaanimad ("When the Wind Shifts"), or "Gway" for short, who was born in 2000. Winona was pregnant when Ralph Nader again invited her to run for vice president in the 2000 national election.

Although Winona was glad about her choice to be part of the Green Party ticket in 1996, it was not an easy decision to run again in 2000. She knew that she would have to find ways to take care of her newborn baby and attend to her family while giving the campaign the full attention it deserved. The Green

Winona stands outside a teepee next to the WELRP office with her son, Gweka-animad, born in 2000. Caring for a newborn did not prevent her from giving speeches and interviews during the campaign season.

Party had grown and planned to be on the ballot in nearly every state. In some states, such as California, there were early projections that the Green Party would win as much as 10 percent of the vote. The 2000 campaign promised to be a much more extensive effort than the 1996 one had been.

In the end, she decided that she could do it. She was encouraged and supported by her family. She also found strength from people whose spirit or memory she carried within her, such as her friend and fellow activist Ingrid Washinawatok El Issa, who had been killed in Columbia in 1999. Ingrid had gone there to help establish an indigenous education program for the Uw'a Indians and to try to prevent oil drilling on their land.

Winona knew that the interests of the oil companies were already strongly represented by the two other parties. She could imagine Ingrid's voice urging her to represent the rights of the people the oil companies had harmed. She could hear Ingrid telling her, "Winona, you gotta run. We need you to do it and speak out for us."

Recently Winona explained her decision to run in 2000 this way: "What I ultimately believe is that if America is going to work as a democracy, and if Indian people are going to be living in this country that surrounds Indian communities, that somehow there has to be a way for those people to have a voice. And this is a part of that process."

With adjustments, she was able to be a mother and a candidate. She campaigned with her baby. At times she nursed him while answering reporters' questions. As an accommodation to her family, she left the Green Party's national convention in Denver a day early so her children did not have to spend extra time cooped up in a hotel.

Her family supported her efforts as well. Together they made it possible for Winona to participate in running a national political campaign without leaving home too often. Her young children became skillful both at helping to take care of the baby and at answering the phone. They could tend to Gway if their mother had to discuss politics with the reporters who were calling from around the country, or if she needed to discuss campaign strategy with people at Green Party offices located far from White Earth. They could also take messages and tell people to call back later if Winona was busy handling the needs of the baby. Because she could stay close to White Earth while campaigning, Winona was able to continue her work with the WELRP and remain involved in the IWN, Honor the Earth, and other projects of great importance to her.

Winona and Ingrid Washinawatok El Issa attend a powwow. As cofounders of the IWN, they worked together to help activists involved in defending indigenous lands, cultures, and people around the globe.

How many women have run for high political office?

In the United States, no woman has yet served as president or vice president. Though a number currently serve in the Senate and as state governors and legislators, very few have run for and won high office. Perhaps this is because it took until 1920 for women in the United States to achieve the right to vote.

The women who have received nominations for vice president in national elections include LaDonna Harris (1980), who ran on the Citizen's Party ticket; Geraldine Ferraro (1984), a congressional representative and Democrat; and Winona LaDuke (1996 and 2000), who ran on the Green Party ticket.

In a number of countries, women have been elected to serve as heads of state. Indira Gandhi of India was one of the first in the twentieth century. Others have included Benazir Bhutto of Pakistan, Corazon Aquino of the Philippines, Mary Robinson of Ireland, and Margaret Thatcher of the United Kingdom.

Geraldine Ferraro addresses the 1984 National Democratic Convention as the party's candidate for vice president.

To some, it might seem impossibly complicated to be doing so many things all at once. In Winona's view, everything that she is doing is interrelated and springs from the same source. As a mother, as a supporter of her local community, as a national political candidate, and as an activist and a voice for indigenous and environmental survival, Winona has created a life composed of many details. Yet these details are closely related. It would not be possible for her to do all these different things if they were not.

Chapter 8

MINOBIMAATISIIWIN— "THE GOOD LIFE"

The closest large city to the White Earth reservation is Fargo, North Dakota. It is a long drive from Fargo to the White Earth boundary, through long miles of level farm fields. Near the end of a wooded road, alongside one of the thousand lakes that Minnesota is famous for, is Winona's house.

It doesn't look like the home of a vice presidential candidate; it looks like any number of the modest homes and summer cabins along the road. In the drive-way are a pickup truck and a family van with a baby seat. From the outside of the house, about the only evidence of the ongoing election campaign is a "Ralph Nader for President" poster in the van's side window.

Winona answers the door with her six-month-old son on her hip and directs a newly arrived visitor into the house. The ordinary domestic scene inside might be taking place in any single-family home in the United States on this midsummer day. The baby needs his cloth diaper changed, and Winona calls over one of the girls to help. Kevin is taking a break from his work to help sort the laundry, while the children and a friend play quietly on the living room floor.

Despite surface appearances, the kitchen and living room are a hub of activity, as messages arrive from the outside world. Two cordless phones ring periodically amid piles of incoming faxes and e-mail printouts that collect on the kitchen table. Throughout the day a steady stream of visitors arrives—journalists, White Earth community members, national campaign staff, White Earth co-workers, and friends. The children come and go from their playing to help out as needed when called on.

Several Green Party volunteers have come up from Minneapolis and are staying overnight at the house. They have been sent by the campaign office to research and compile data on particular policy issues. Their work will help Winona prepare for her upcoming public appearances. In the absence of the multimillion-dollar campaign budgets of the Democrats and Republicans, the Green Party functions remarkably well using the work of unpaid staff, many of them college students.

Winona often organizes events, makes schedules, and gives interviews from her telephone at home.

A reporter interviews Winona for a news story. Winona voices concern about the failure of the Republicans or Democrats to address the needs of most people in the United States. Her comments are thoughtful and fully articulated. They are also, at times, candid and humorously stated.

As a journalist herself, she understands how to say interesting things that can be quoted in a news story. She keeps a friendly but responsible tone with journalists, and lightens the seriousness of the occasion without distracting from the importance of what she is saying. Her own humor and ease with herself are relaxing to be around. She takes an occasional break during the interview to interact with her newborn, blowing on his cheeks and making him open his toothless mouth in a smiling, silent laugh.

Later a group of women come by to discuss ideas and strategy for a quilting business on White Earth. The "Aunties," elderly women of the community, are excited about the arrival of a high-speed quilting machine that was secured with money from a grant. Robynn Carter, WELRP community organizer, has also been trying to secure the use of a comfortable house with a kitchen for quilters to work in. After the group leaves, Winona explains that this is a project to honor some of the older women in the community and provide a showcase for their skills. "It gives them a boost because it shows them that somebody cares," Winona says.

On the wall above a writing desk near her kitchen table is a cartoon. Its caption is a twist on the slogan "Think Globally, Act Locally." The cartoon is a reflec-

Margaret Smith, a White Earth elder, uses the new high-speed quilting machine provided by the WELRP.

tion of Winona's ability to enjoy humor while still having ambitious ideals. It reads: "Think Galactically, Act Globally."

Winona does seem to be able to move back and forth instantly and comfortably from the local to the global, and sometimes reach beyond, to something larger than everyday human life. Someone asked her how all her diverse roles were related. How could she be a candidate, a mother, a wife, a program director of two nonprofit agencies, an activist, speaker, novelist, and journalist? What kept her going and linked all these many activities?

She paused for a long time, as if looking inside before coming up with her answer. "There's an Ojibwe word, *minobimaatisiiwin,* which means 'the good life,' and that's the cultural framework that I live by in aspiring to live that good life."

She went on to say that "the good life" is a state of fairness and balance on many levels. On the personal level, the good life means having a healthy family and set of extended family relations. Children need love and care. They also need to be taught and given responsibility. The members of a family need to honor and support each other.

On another level, the good life is mirrored in the relationships of a healthy community. For this reason, work done to preserve culture, honor elders, and support the education of young people in the local environment are examples of what leads to *minobimaatisiiwin* as well.

Promoting fair trade and economic justice within and among nations brings this balance to the world at large. And at this global level, as at the others, the

Winona stretches out her arms as Gway takes his first steps.

good life extends beyond the human community to include living things in nature such as trees, because, she said, trees are also our relatives.

"So you try to live a good life and to have all of us live a good healthy life. And I say that that is it, for me—the striving for that in the simple way."

In Winona's pursuit of the simple way—of balance in her community and in the world—she tends to place emphasis on the importance of others, rather than call attention to herself. This is a quality that helps explain why she has been so successful at helping to build cooperative relationships with other activists and at creating positive organizations.

What may sometimes be harder to see, because she is not one to tout her own importance, is the uniqueness of what she has done and continues to do. She hasn't shown an interest in getting attention

Winona's family and circle of friends has continued to grow. Sitting together on the couch at her house at White Earth are, from left, Ajuawak Kapashesit (upside down), Kevin Gasco, Jon Martin (upside down), Winona with Gway on her lap, Ashley Martin (upside down), Lorna Haynes, and Waseyabin Kapashesit.

or wealth for herself. These things have never seemed important to her.

Her mother, Betty LaDuke, remembers, "I was really moved when she got the Reebok Human Rights Award and turned around and then used the twenty thousand dollars, which she could have used herself a million times over, to start the White Earth Land Recovery Project."

Winona urges others to act within a larger awareness as well. In her view, natural law does not permit an unbalanced relationship between the self and others. For example, the excessive consumption of energy and materials by industrialized nations will eventually deplete the earth for everyone else. A greater balance needs to be established between what is taken and what is given, so that the earth can support everyone. Members of indigenous cultures tend to be aware of this. One reason is that they are living in a tradition that is based on a close, and often practical, relationship with the natural environment. The Anishinaabeg need the forest because it supplies them with plants and animals they use to survive. They would no sooner cut down acres of trees than they would burn down their own houses.

The other reason is that indigenous people, because of their historic lack of a voice and rights in the U.S. political system, have often been at the frontlines of ecological disaster. Unable to defend themselves and their lands, they have witnessed firsthand the destruction of the environment.

As Winona understands, however, the day is already here when the problems of Native peoples are those of the whole world. She quotes Danny

Billie of the Seminole tribe, who have traditionally lived in the endangered Florida Everglades.

When asked by a reporter if the Seminoles could survive, Billie reminded the reporter that the Seminoles are no different from anyone else. "What we want is what you need, too. It's what this society needs, if they want to stay alive on this earth. . . . Not only do we want to survive as we are, I'm pretty sure that you want to survive as who you are, too."

If the people of the world are to survive as they are, it will require a shift in thinking. People in the industrialized world need to learn from indigenous peoples. In particular, they need to understand that in order to live in accordance with natural law, there must be a balance between what is taken and what is given back. To achieve long-term survival and well-being, it is important to take only what is needed and leave the rest. Otherwise there is imbalance. Today, on a global scale, the lack of responsibility toward the earth has created an imbalance that endangers human survival.

"In my community, it's a cultural value that you are responsible for that which you take," Winona says. "I'm not going to tell the people in Washington, D.C., that they should pray before they go buy their lettuce. But I like to know where my food comes from. In the era of globalization, it is increasingly frightening that some people do not have a relationship to the chain of custody of these products."

The well-being of the earth and future generations requires a more conscious and responsible relationship between ourselves and our impact on the natural world. The first practical step to restoring

Today Winona continues to speak out about the causes that have motivated her activism. She remains confident that Native Americans and environmentalists will prevail in their efforts to protect the earth. "We're not going anywhere." she says, "And we will not give up."

balance is to take back local responsibility for the primary sources of pollution—energy production and agriculture.

In Winona's view, "The more you can have some relationship to energy or food production, the better. It is the externalizing of production that makes us operate by remote control." Operating by remote control means giving away our responsibility to corporations and government. When energy is produced far away, for example, it is easier to remain ignorant or unconcerned about who had to suffer to make it possible. It is also easier to remain unaware of the harmful effects that energy production may be having on the earth, our own bodies, or those of children and families in our local community.

"The ethical consideration," Winona says, "is to be responsible somehow for those things you take into your life." This responsibility can place us in the middle of a conflict between the world as it is and the world as it should be.

Winona has spent her adult life as part of a movement to protect the earth and give more power to Native people. She has tried, however, to keep in mind that those who oppose her are worthy of respect as well.

She cites the Anishinaabeg teaching of "Most Honored Enemy." "What it means," she explains, "is even those you might disagree with, still you treat as an honorable foe. Because in a lot of cases they aren't necessarily bad people. They just have a different view of things." This perspective also has a practical side. "I like to be treated in an honorable manner by them," she says.

The struggle to halt ecological destruction and rejuvenate Native lands demands patience. Winona knows that indigenous people face many challenges, but believes that they have an advantage over the forces of short-term interests. "We're not going anywhere," she said. "And we will not give up."

As for her own view, she maintains a long-term, determined perspective. "Things take a long time to fix," she says. "If it takes a hundred years to get back the land, then that is the way it is." She recognizes that her ability to maintain a positive spirit and take constructive action is a right that she can choose not to surrender.

In her vision and in the example of her activism and leadership, Winona LaDuke evokes the great traditions of Native American culture.

"She's rejuvenating us," said Ken Bellanger, former chairman of the Minnesota American Indian

Chamber of Commerce, who witnessed the effects of the WELRP on the White Earth community. "She's a role model to your young Indian women. In the Indian way, the great majority of great leaders were women. . . . The power in our communities and the power behind our culture lies in people like Winona."

Winona herself is quick to point out that the handprint she is credited with leaving on White Earth is not hers alone. "Our collective handprint, is perhaps what I would say, because I haven't done anything myself. But I would say that I've worked with different people and we've been able to create something on this reservation that a lot of people are interested in coming out to see." Specifically, she attributes the achievements of the WELRP to the many people who have given their commitment, courage, and innovation to the project.

Winona LaDuke says that the source of her power and activism is her spiritual belief. Like many Native people, she believes that "power emanates from nature—that the wellspring of all life is in nature and in our relationships with creation and the Creator. I believe that natural power, natural law, is the highest and most significant form of power."

What needs to be changed, in Winona's view, is our belief that power comes from money and force. "We women in particular give our power to big companies that determine what we wear, how we think, what popular culture is, what we eat. We relinquish the gift of our individuality to big corporations. I don't believe that giving our power to big corporations is responsible," she says.

Winona's greatest hope for young people, and particularly girls, is that they can recognize the true source of power in nature, and that they can realize their potential. In this way, she says, they will be able to "determine their futures and recover some of who they are."

CHRONOLOGY

1959   Winona LaDuke is born on August 18 in Los
            Angeles, California.

1965   Vincent and Betty LaDuke separate. Winona and
            her mother move to Ashland, Oregon.

1966   Betty LaDuke marries entomologist Peter
            Westigard.

1977   Winona enters Harvard University. She travels to
            Geneva, Switzerland, to speak at a United Nations
            conference on the problems of indigenous people.

1978–81   At various times, Winona works with
            environmental activists in the Southwest.

1982–83   Winona graduates from Harvard. She attends the
            Massachusetts Institute of Technology (MIT)
            Community Fellows Program.

1983   Winona returns to the White Earth reservation.

1985   The Indigenous Women's Network is founded.

1987   Legal efforts to recover White Earth land are
            rejected in court.

1988   Winona marries Randy Kapashesit, a leader of the
            Cree tribe in northern Ontario. Their daughter,
            Waseyabin, is born.

1989   Winona wins the Reebok Human Rights Award.
            With the $20,000 prize, she establishes the White
            Earth Land Recovery Project. Winona completes a
            master's degree at Antioch University.

1990   Winona's son Ajuawak is born.

1992   Winona and her husband are separated. Her father,
            Vincent, dies.

1994   The James Bay II hydroelectric project is halted.

	Winona is named one of fifty "Leaders for the Future" by *Time* magazine.
1995	The Honor the Earth tour raises more than $250,000 for forty-one grassroots organizations.
1996	Winona accepts the Green Party nomination for vice president. She campaigns with Ralph Nader, the Green Party candidate for president.
1997	*Last Standing Woman* is published. The second major Honor the Earth tour takes place.
1999	*All Our Relations: Native Struggles for Land and Life* is published.
2000	Winona's son Gwekaanimad is born. Winona accepts her second Green Party nomination for vice president with Ralph Nader as her running mate.

GLOSSARY

activist A person who works to call problems to the attention of government officials or the public.

Anishinaabeg (Ah-nish-in-AH-beg) Native American tribe (also known as the Ojibwe) of the Minnesota and Great Lakes area.

civil disobedience Nonviolent method of protesting a law or government policy.

clear-cut To indiscriminately take down every tree in a forested area.

economist A person who studies how wealth is created and exchanged.

entomologist A scientist who studies insects.

giiwe (GI-way) Ojibwe word meaning "going home."

indigenous Belonging to, or native to, a particular geographical area.

midwife Someone skilled at assisting a pregnant woman as she is giving birth.

minobimaatisiiwin (min-o-bi-MAH-ti-SEE-win) Ojibwe word meaning "the good life."

racism Unfair treatment of people based on racial or ethnic differences.

reservation Land designated by the U.S. government for habitation by Native Americans.

Acronyms

BIA Bureau of Indian Affairs

IWN Indigenous Women's Network

UN United Nations

WELRP White Earth Land Recovery Project

FURTHER READING

Books by Winona LaDuke

All Our Relations: Native Struggles for Land and Life. Cambridge, Mass.: South End Press, 1999.
Last Standing Woman. Stillwater, Minn.: Voyageur Press, 1997.

Books on the Minnesota Ojibwe

Treuer, Anton, translator. *Living Our Language: Ojibwe Tales and Oral Histories*. St. Paul: Minnesota Historical Society Press, 2001
Vannote, Vance, and Janet Pratt. *Women of White Earth: Photographs and Interviews*. Minneapolis: University of Minnesota Press, 1999.

Books on Native American Issues and the Environment

Caduto, Michael J., and Joseph Bruchac. *Keepers of the Earth: Native American Stories and Environmental Activities for Children*. Golden, Colo.: Fulcrum, 1988.
Elkington, John. *Going Green: A Kids' Handbook to Saving the Planet*. New York: Puffin Books, 1990.
Gravelle, Karen. *Soaring Spirits: Conversations with Native American Teens*. New York: Franklin Watts, 1995.
Smith, Paul Chaat, and Robert Allen Warrior. *Like a Hurricane: The Indian Movement from Alcatraz to Wounded Knee*. New York: New Press, 1997.
Spangenburg, Ray, and Diane K. Moser. *The American Indian Experience*. New York: Facts on File, 1997.
Weaver, Jace, and Russell Means, eds. *Defending Mother Earth: Native American Perspectives on Environmental Justice*. Maryknoll, N.Y.: Orbis Books, 1996.
Wilson, James. *The Earth Shall Weep: A History of Native America*. New York: Atlantic Monthly Press, 1999.

Internet Sites

Green Party
(http://www.greenparty.org)

Greenpeace USA
(http://www.greenpeaceusa.org/)

Honor the Earth
http://www.honorearth.com/music. html

Indigenous Women's Network
(http://www.honorearth.com/iwn/aboutiwn.html)

White Earth Land Recovery Project
(http://www.welrp.org)

Film/Video

Power. A documentary film about the James Bay II hydroelectric project. Directed by Magnus Isacsson. 77 min. Telefilm Canada and the Ontario Film Development Corporation in association with the National Film Board of Canada, 1996.

INDEX

Page numbers in *italic* type indicate photo captions

Acknowledgments

The author wishes to thank:

Kevin Gasco, Winona LaDuke and family, Betty LaDuke, WELRP staff members, Robynn Carter, Robert Tibbetts, Juanita Lindsay, Cindy Lindsay, Florence Goodman, Donna Cahill, and Lori Pourier of the Indigenous Women's Network; Feminist Press colleagues Livia Tenzer, Jean Casella, Florence Howe, Lisa London, Raquel Baetz, Amanda Hamlin, Heather McMaster, and Dayna Navaro; the students, families, and alumni of Class C-4; teaching colleagues Mangala Jagadeesh, Barb Fukushima, Sarah Bing-Owen, Linda Gianesin, Terez Waldoch, Gus Sayer, Ron Bell, Karen Lowe, and many other inspiring teachers at Wildwood Elementary; and also for varied forms of support and inspiration, Sander Schwartz, Joyce Goodman, E. I. Schwartz, Matilda and Jack Goodman, Tom Neal, Calvin Hernton, Judy Coven, John S. Mayher, Alan Zeigler, Nancy Larson Shapiro, Neil Ortenberg, and Ziporah Hildebrandt. Most especially, to B. and to Bear, with boundless gratitude, beatitude, respect, and love.

Picture Credits

Courtesy of Kevin Brown and John Ratzloff: 82; Corbis Images: 25, 31, 38, 43, 46, 56, 65, 91; Rick Dahms: 69; Flying Eagle Woman Fund: 90; Ilka Hartman, copyright (c) 2001: 32; Betty LaDuke: 29, 35; Winona LaDuke: 18, 23, 24, 33, 39, 51, 54, 57, 58, 61, 62, 66, 68, 88, 94; Keri Pickett: 71, 77, 83, 93, 95, 96, 99; John Ratzloff: 12; Michael Silverstone: 89; Voyageur Press, copyright © 1997: 52.

About the Author

Michael Silverstone is a writer whose previously published works for young people include biographies of Comanche activist LaDonna Harris, youth advocate Luis J. Rodríguez, and Nobel Peace Prize-winner Rigoberta Menchú of Guatemala (*Rigoberta Menchú: Defending Human Rights in Guatemala*, The Feminist Press, 1999). He is an elementary school teacher in Amherst, Massachusetts.